THE SPIDER:
THE SPIDER AND THE EYELESS LEGION

# THE SPIDER
## MASTER OF MEN!

# THE SPIDER AND
# THE EYELESS LEGION

*By Grant Stockbridge*

POPULAR PUBLICATIONS • 2023

PUBLISHING HISTORY

"The Spider and the Eyeless Legion" originally appeared in the October, 1939 (Vol. 19, No. 1) issue of *The Spider* magazine. Copyright 2023 by Argosy Communications, Inc. All rights reserved.

# CHAPTER 1
## THE SPIDER SLIPS

I N SPITE of the neat silk mask, the man in evening dress did not look like a safecracker. But his deft gloved hands had taken some sixty thousand dollars, in large bills, from the looted strongbox and were rapidly stowing them away into prepared pockets beneath the tailored snugness of his white vest!

That job finished, he slipped a thin platinum cigarette lighter from his pocket, thumbed open the base and leaned forward to press it against the face of the safe. It was while he stood there, a suggestion of lithe power in the arch of the back, that he caught the stealthy opening of a door in the suite's outer office....

He whipped about with quick, feral tension. There was a sharp contraction in the cords of his columnar throat; the smile on his lips became taut. Behind him, where he had touched the door of the safe, was revealed the reason. Etched there in rich vermilion, standing out boldly against the black metal, was... *the seal of the Spider!*

That seal labeled the man in the mask the most hunted fugitive in the entire United States, sought alike by a dogged police and a viciously frightened underworld—and it labeled him, too, the greatest humanitarian the world had ever known! It was a true identification.

With long silent strides the Spider, who in another identity was the wealthy clubman and sportsman, Richard Wentworth,

They slaved in the
sweat-shops of hell!

crossed to the heavy oaken door that shut off the outer office. His gloved fingers played soundlessly over the lock, made sure of the fastenings. Then he turned his back upon it—and opened a costly case to select a cigarette! Casually lighting it, he strolled back to continue his calm perusal of the safe's contents!

Despite his iron self-discipline in the face of danger, the Spider had been unable to control that first nervous reaction to discovery. Six months before, he would not have needed the reassurance of examining a door he knew to be locked, but in these straitened days, when police sought him both as Wentworth and as the Spider, they kept up a relentless pressure. Doggedly, sometimes weeks late, they crossed his back trail and, ever and again, they flushed him from the hideout in the slums to which he had been forced to retreat. For once, too, the underworld had joined forces with the law. He was one man against whom the most tight-lipped felon would inform—if he did not shoot the Spider down upon recognition! Yet Wentworth's only crime was the service of humanity, according to his own conscience and his own heart.

Still unhurried, Wentworth turned with a sheaf of papers toward a secretary's noiseless typewriter in a corner of the office. His eyes glanced toward the door and amusement lingered in their blue-gray depths. More than one man out there; probably the police. Well, the door would hold for a while against assault—and there was still work to be done for the humanity he served, selflessly and without other reward than the work itself....

AT THE typewriter, he snicked in a sheet of paper with gloved fingers, concentrated on the phrasing of the message. He heard the metallic whisper of the doorknob being turned, the smothered creak of pressure against the panel, and he nodded at the confirmation of his thought. Yes, certainly, the police! Even the most bungling of sneak thieves would make less noise.

Not that the identity of this sneaking ambuscade mattered. When they saw the seal, the police would shoot him down without mercy... and, even to save his life, the Spider would not fire on the forces of the law! Actually, he did not have a gun! He moved his cigarette to the side of the desk and ashes spilled across the broadcloth of his trousers. Wentworth swore under his breath, angry at himself for that slight betrayal of nervousness.

Another man would have fled in panic long ago, even if it had been merely capture, and not death, that waited outside the door... but the Spider scorned himself for a tremor! It was typical of this avenger whom even his enemies had named, grudgingly, Master of Men.

Abruptly, the police outside abandoned their stealth. A gun butt hammered on the door and a man's voice rasped in challenge.

"Open up, there! It's the police. You're surrounded. Come on, open up... or do you want it the hard way?"

A mocking smile crossed Wentworth's lips and he cried out in imitation of a frightened woman, his voice lifted, shrill.

"Oh—oh, the police... Oh, *John!*"

There was a startled silence outside the door and, in that moment's surcease, Wentworth swiftly drummed out the message on which he had determined:

John Lauder,

You obtained today the acquittal of Frank Rocker, whom you know to be guilty of the murder of Officer Shea. Rocker will pay for his crime; and I have taken from you the receipts of your own crime. This is your first and last warning. It might not be wise for you to transgress again. There is, this experience should teach you, a justice that does not wait on the law, whose technicalities you know so well—and employ so treacherously.

There was no signature, but with the Spider seal on the door, none was necessary. He tucked the paper into the safe where it could not be missed, and turned toward the door. It was a man's deep voice he used now while irony tilted his brows.

"What the devil do you mean!" he demanded roughly of the unseen police. "Forcing your way like this into my office!"

There was a mutter of voices outside the door. Then the man who had first spoken began some explanations... and stubbornly demanded that the door be opened. Wentworth moved quietly to the desk and picked up his cigarette for a final puff, strode to the open window. He flicked the cigarette into space, mounted the sill. Four stories below was the flat roof of Carnegie Hall, where a concert was in progress. His seat check was in his pocket, his silk hat and dapper cape in the checkroom....

His fingers reached to the window cleaner's hook, set deeply in the masonry, and found a light line of silk. It was scarcely larger than a pencil, but, nevertheless, had a tested strength of more than seven hundred pounds—the Spider's web. Here was his line of escape... but Wentworth paused there, gazing out over the sparkling panorama of New York's night skyline, though behind him police axes were thudding into the office door!

There was a smile in Wentworth's keen eyes at this moment. He loved the great brawling city spread beneath him, loved all its garishness and chicanery, its occasional moments of austere beauty and human surprise. But the smile hardened. The city's very largeness bred its vermin of crime, and it was the Spider's task—and pleasure—to exterminate them!

A louder crash at the door hurried his movements a little. He twisted the silken line about his arms and took a loop about a hard thigh. Damn it, his nerves were like taut violin strings. He must somehow break free of this battle against the underworld long enough to clear himself of the charges of murder which the police pressed against Richard Wentworth. If his friend, Stanley Kirkpatrick, recovered his health sufficiently to resume office as police commissioner, these charges would not stand a day. Not because Kirkpatrick would shirk his duty even for Wentworth, but because the charges were basically incapable of proof. Of the crimes with which Richard Wentworth was charged in his own name, Wentworth was innocent! And harassed as he was, forced into hiding, the Spider was hampered in his battles against crime.

WENTWORTH DROPPED to the sill, swung off into space and began to slip soundlessly down the face of the building. Behind him, he heard the oaken door begin to splinter. Had his bitter self-discipline forced him to delay too long? But safety was below. The police would not find him once he had mingled again with the *haut monde* of the concert. The smile

once more moved his strongly chis-
eled lips—and froze there! He was
barely two stories above the roof of
the Hall when he saw the moving
shadows of men. The police in the office had spoken the truth.
He was surrounded!

Even as the full realization of his predicament—pinned like
an impaled beetle against the wall—struck into Wentworth's
consciousness, his keen brain was leaping toward a solution of
his dilemma. He could not check for a single moment his even
descent of the web. That would instantly betray to the men below
the fact that he had spotted them. By continuing to drop toward
their waiting guns, he could gain some few seconds! His eyes
jerked toward the second-story window just below and to one
side. That was his only chance, but the guns of the police were
very close. At this range, they could not miss. His only chance....

Wentworth thrust fiercely against the side of the building.
His body swung out, made a short, accelerating arc—and he
slammed back-first against the window! No time to open it;
no need! The impact drove in the glass in a thousand knife-
edged shards. He felt their swift hot touch on his cheek, then
his groping feet found the floor. He flung himself violently aside,
barely before a deluge of lead poured through the opening. The
room was filled with the shriek and whine of bullets; the ceiling
pulverized. White dust puffed downward.

Back flat against the wall, Wentworth went methodically
about freeing himself from the silken line which, because of its
thinness, he had had to twist several times about arms and leg.

A frown was tight upon his mask-hidden forehead. He was cut off from his only sure refuge in Carnegie Hall. The anonymity of formal clothing, which would have been a protection then, now became a terrific handicap. Men in full evening dress did not run hatless through the city streets. The frown gave way to a brief smile of self-mockery. He was a little premature, wasn't he? He had not yet reached the street!

Free of the silk web, Wentworth dragged the line down hard on a rim of broken glass and looped the free end swiftly in his fist. Bullets still hammered against the ceiling. A ricochet shot screamed viciously close. The office was fogged with white dust. In the halls, the shouts of men and the urgent slap of running feet told him that the police inside the building were closing in! Dimly, words came to his ears, and he knew that they had found his seal on the safe door. Fiercely, the shouts rang out:

"The Spider! It's the Spider! *Shoot to kill!*"

Keeping carefully clear of the line of fire, Wentworth raced to another window that opened on the back of the building, flung it up. From the roof below, guns hurled their fiery lances toward him. Wentworth swung aside violently, and his heart pounded with mounting excitement. This was no ordinary thief-trap that had been set. A score of men lay in ambush for him! Slowly, grimness built a cold smile in his eyes. This strong force was a harsh compliment, but it meant one thing surely: The police had somehow known that the man in Lauder's office was the Spider!

Even in the swift moment while he whirled from the window to try the last exit from the office—the door—Wentworth recorded that thought in his fertile brain. This tip-off could mean only one thing: an underworld plot against the Spider! And always, in the past, such activities had heralded the rise of a new criminal monster intent on inflicting his greedy will upon the people! When the Spider was free of this trap....

Dashing toward the last exit, Wentworth strained every sense to determine the whereabouts of the police. If they were already in the hallway, waiting... His hand closed on the knob, and an oath leaped to his lips. Against the ground glass of the door panel, he saw the shadow of a uniformed man! He ducked to the right and the glass was driven inward in the same instant. Through the smashed glass, the policeman began to pour a frantic stream of lead!

The concussion of the blasts deafened Wentworth, sent him reeling headlong against the wall. Even as he staggered, he went into action! His left hand clamped on the cop's gun-wrist and dragged him forward. The silken line flew from his right, blindingly into the man's face, a split second before he crashed a pile-driver right to the cop's jaw. No pause to see the effect of that blow! The Spider heaved the limp cop backward and leaped after him through the broken door-pane. An instant later, he had caught up the man's uniform and cap and gun, heaved the unconscious form to his shoulders and was sprinting along the corridor!

FOOTSTEPS WERE pounding overhead and the first hard clatter of racing men hit the metal stairs one story above. The others were closer than he had thought! Wentworth pivoted in mid-stride, darted toward an office door. The captured gun in his right fist spat once. The lock was blasted to fragments and his shoulder drove the door open. As that door eased shut, another policeman took the last long leap down the stairs and skated across the hallway, caromed from the wall on his shoulder. He sprinted toward the office which Wentworth had left an instant before. A crowded wedge of other cops careened in his wake, skidded to a cautious halt beside the shattered panel, guns ready in their fists.

While they crouched, ready for the kill, another door farther down the hallway opened and a man in a police uniform coat and cap edged out into the open. It was a curious thing that this policeman wore patent-leather shoes, and a white, formal tie! He reached the stairway that led downward, passed it, turned his back toward the cops. Then he began to slap his feet down heavily in an echoing run.

"This way!" he shouted hoarsely. "This way! *He went down the stairs!*"

The cop in patent-leather opera pumps waved an urgent arm and leaped down the stairs. For a puzzled moment, the other officers watched him, then they darted in his wake.

"Shoot him, Bill!" they chorused. "Shoot, if you see him! It's the Spider!"

Two flights ahead of the police, the man in patent-leather shoes was taking the steps in great leaps that would be possible only to a man at the peak of his physical strength and with the perfectly timed reflexes of a championship fencer. Yet he had time for a brief, bitter smile. Wentworth had no doubt that, in his parti-uniform, he could escape from the building, but where would he go then? It was becoming increasingly clear that his

11

RICHARD WENTWORTH .

disguise must have been penetrated, and everywhere he would be hounded by that hoarsely enraged shout, *"Kill the Spider!"* Yes, Wentworth knew his moment of bitterness. It was not that he hoped for reward in his service, but to be condemned unheard by the men he most helped....

Gradually, the police were falling behind. The incredible pace that the Spider set would have distanced champions. On the second floor, Wentworth whirled to the right and sprinted past a half-dozen doors to whirl at last and drive his shoulder hard against the seventh. He slammed the door, reached the window in three long bounds and flung it upward. As he had calculated, the marquee of the building was just beneath. In a moment he had crossed it and was peering cautiously over the lighted sign that formed its front edge… and he chuckled softly then, mockery tilting his brows. Here was a possibility!

Just below him was a limousine that he recognized. It belonged to his old friend, Kirkpatrick, but now it was being used by his fiercest enemy—the acting commissioner of police, Sanford Dane!

The Spider, as usual, had found the perfect means of escape!

With a single, smooth effort, Wentworth leaped to the roof of the car and dropped to the street lightly beside the driver's seat! The chauffeur whipped about a startled face, and his hand clawed for an underarm gun! But the Spider had anticipated that. Before the man's hand had more than started for the holster, Wentworth's clenched left pistoned through the open window and caught the driver flush on the jaw. As the man's

head wrenched about under that knockout punch, Wentworth whipped open the door.

It was the work of an instant to transfer the chauffeur to the dark tonneau of the car… and take his vacated place behind the steering wheel!

The motor leaped instantly to powerful life under his touch and he had time to make a more thorough examination of the street. As his first swift glance had shown him, there were many uniformed police about, but their eyes were all pinned upon the side entrance of the building from which Wentworth had just escaped. There was a stiffness of horror in their poses, and as Wentworth saw the reason, he felt tightness creep into his own cheeks!

From that entrance, policemen were staggering in a pitiful agonized file—and their hands were clawing frantically at their eyes!

There were five of these stumbling, blinded men and, abruptly, one of them uttered a strangled cry and began to run! He slammed against a light post, wheeled about dazedly as the shock whipped his hands away from his eyes. He flung his head madly from side to side. He lifted clenched fists to beat at his forehead, at his own eyes—and began to run again, a few quick prancing steps one way, then another, bending double, straightening, dancing in agony; and, intolerably, he began to scream!

Wentworth swore between his teeth and his hand hesitated on the gearshift. In heaven's name, what was happening here? His first thought had been that someone had dropped a tear-gas bomb, but no tear gas ever made could cause such agony as this. Besides, tear gas brought always a strangled coughing, and there was no such indication. Perhaps....

WENTWORTH'S THOUGHTS broke off in sheer dazed horror, for the screaming policeman collided sharply with the brick wall of the building, and did not recoil. Instead, he stood there and beat his face against the stone wall, furiously, with violent strength, in an agony past all bearing and all belief!

Wentworth's hand was on the door. The necessity for escape was forgotten, for he knew now what was happening in this Hell of pain. Fleetingly, he had guessed that some new underworld power was at work. Now he knew it! This—this horror he was witnessing—was the work of that new power. And, daringly, with characteristic lack of thought for his own danger, the Spider was going to combat it! But even as he flung wide the door, he became aware of a brawny giant of a man plunging toward the limousine at a hard run! It took only that single glance—a glimpse of the man's uncovered head with its blunt skull scarcely covered by close-clipped hair—for Wentworth to recognize Acting Commissioner Sanford Dane!

"You there, Mike!" he shouted. "Throw that radio switch! Get every ambulance in reach! Quick! Tell them, bring everything they can think of to treat eyes! Those men are going blind!"

Coolly, Wentworth threw the switch, picked up the microphone. "Commissioner Dane calling headquarters," he snapped. "Commissioner Dane calling headquarters. Rush all ambulances to Fifty-Seventh and Seventh. Police blinded by unknown gas. Bring eye lotions. Pilocarpine. Atropine. Come in, headquarters!"

Dane's fists hit the side of the car with a jar. He clawed at the door handle. "Get that radio going...."

"Repeating for headquarters," Wentworth said quietly, into the microphone, and began steadily to repeat the message which headquarters had acknowledged in part. Out of his eye corners, he saw Sanford Dane thrust his square, hardboned head through the window, saw the flare of his eyes as he realized that  the man behind the wheel was not his chauffeur. But the Spider's steady voice did not falter. It was like the Spider that even in this moment when death threatened at the hands of the police, he should bend every effort to help the stricken soldiers of the law.

Dane's voice came out hoarsely. "Mike... You aren't Mike. Why, damn you...."

Dane's powerful right arm stabbed toward Wentworth's throat. His left clawed for a revolver.

"This way, men!" he shouted. "Here he is! I've caught the Spider!"

Wentworth ripped out the last of the message to headquarters, and swayed backward from the grasp of the commissioner's hand. His right stabbed out to seize the man's gun wrist, and pin it immovably to his chest.

"Just a minute, Dane," he said harshly. "If you care nothing for your men going blind there, you might permit a criminal to take care of them!"

At that instant, he caught acknowledgment of the order from headquarters and his feet did two things in the same split second. He kicked the accelerator to the floor, let the clutch slam out... and thrust Dane violently backward! Dane's fists rapped the side of the car and, as the limousine surged forward, Wentworth caught a swift glimpse of him in the rear-vision mirror.

Dane was thrown, reeling, to the sidewalk. He was up in an instant, gun in hand, shouting orders... The view flicked sideways, was cut off by a brick wall as Wentworth whipped around a corner. The motor was roaring with magnificent power. Deftly, one hand on the wheel, Wentworth controlled the limousine while he lifted the microphone once more to see that the last letter of his instructions to the police, via Dane, was obeyed!

There was no humor in Wentworth's eyes now; only grimness in the mobile line of his solidly chiseled lips. No man enjoyed better than he a clash with powerful foes, even though life itself be the stake. But this was beyond battle-joy. Innocent people were suffering... and the Spider must once more take the lone and harassed trail of justice. There would be no more joy in this contest for him—until the man who had caused these things was brought to the bar of justice from which there was no appeal: the unerring guns of the Spider!

His mind was clicking with the cold precision that made Wentworth so dreaded in the underworld haunts of crime. He scarcely heard the police sirens that already were yelping on his trail as he swung the heavy limousine through the traffic. The police would blame the Spider for what had happened to those tortured officers of the law. But it was not that which brought the hard frown of concentration to his forehead. It was the fact that someone had deliberately plotted to the end that he should be blamed!

Wentworth bent more alertly over the wheel, jammed the siren button down and held it while the limousine gained momentum down Fifth Avenue. Police on post sprang out to part the torrent of traffic. At another time, the thought that the police were helping his escape would have brought a mocking smile to the Spider's lips, but this was too deadly serious. There could be no question now that criminals had somehow penetrated his disguise, and tipped the police to trap him—yet no one on earth had known his plans for the night!

SINCE HE had been driven into hiding as Richard Wentworth, his once impregnable home blown to bits by criminals, he had been entirely alone. Even the woman who alone shared all his secrets, who alone held his love, did not know where he was or in what disguise he lurked. And she, Nita van Sloan, had all his former comrades-in-arms at her command. That had been necessary to protect them from the murder charge that Dane had filed against him as a result of the destruction of Wentworth's home.

A score of police had died in that explosion, and Dane persisted in holding him responsible though Wentworth had shouted a frantic warning to the imperiled men at immediate risk of his own life! He was completely alone—yet this new criminal had penetrated his secret.

It meant that his disguise as Casimir Belotti, an impoverished street musician who earned a precarious living playing

in the slums, had been discovered. He must have been followed, when he left his home this night, his destination discovered, and the trap set afterward. There was no other explanation! But it meant more than that. In order for this new criminal to know that Casimir Belotti was the Spider, men must have followed Wentworth in the Spider's disguise after some recent foray against the underworld—and instead of killing him, had spared his life for some crooked purpose!

Wentworth's lips twisted in a slow, cold smile, and the fires that lurked in his blue-gray eyes sparkled with determined anger. By these maneuvers, the criminals had saved him a great deal of trouble! They knew him, and they would come for him—and the Spider would be obliging!

Wentworth whipped the car eastward off Fifth Avenue and began to drill toward the slums that flanked the river. He had one sanctum of the Spider left, a small individual garage hidden on an alley. This, too, must be known to the new criminal, for it had been there that Wentworth changed to evening dress! Either there, or at the home of Casimir Belotti, these criminals would come for him. At the thought of their welcome, Wentworth laughed once, sharply, and the sound was flat and mocking and full of menace. It was the laughter of the Spider!

Wentworth swung the limousine into an alley and left it there. For a block, he ran on silent feet, then he began to swing briskly along as if he were a policeman bent on duty.

The brawling of the slums was dying to a sleepy muttering, punctuated only by the occasional wail of a child, the clatter of a distant El train. The whimpering quest of the police radio cars swept past and died away; presently began to swing toward him again. But Wentworth had reached the alley that led to his sanctum. He loosened the captured police revolver in its holster, but did not check his steady approach. If it was here that the criminals lay in wait, it was better to seem unsuspicious!

Wentworth's eyes quested swiftly ahead, probing the shadows squatting against the walls, shuttling over black, empty windows—and found nothing. Had they been too sure of victory in the Lauder office to set a trap here? Wentworth reached a point opposite the garage doors. He weighed the gun in his fist and, behind him, he fluttered a hand back and forth in a curious rhythm across an aperture in the brick wall through which a hidden mechanism threw a ray of infrared light. The doors of the garage swung smoothly open, a brilliant light flashed on for an instant… The garage was empty!

Without hesitation, Wentworth sprang into the garage and the doors slid shut. His swift investigation revealed no trap, nowhere for a man to hide… yet a feeling of danger persisted. Certainly the attack would come! Wentworth shrugged, laid his revolver carefully on the floor as he knelt over a small secret trapdoor. He must give the criminals their chance. He would go back to the dingy room of Casimir Belotti!

A small make-up mirror, a tray of the implements of disguise, and Wentworth's deft hands set swiftly to work. For an instant after he had stripped off his disguise, the clear, strong features of Richard Wentworth were visible—then a lotion sallowed the tan, firm skin, blocked out the generous lips. He changed the narrow-bridged, intelligent nose to a beak, then caught up the sober worn clothing of his disguise, clasped a violin, left hidden here, beneath his arm. He moved with an arthritic stiffness as he accustomed himself to the new identity, and his back was bent. He tucked the revolver into his waistband... and Casimir Belotti was ready for the street!

ALL THE long, slow walk to the lodging house, Wentworth was conscious of the unrelenting pressure of danger, but he reached home without event and, undressing, extinguished the light as if for sleep. He lay, then, with the gun beneath his fist and a cold, waiting smile upon his lips....

Wentworth had no consciousness of sleepiness, nor of drowsing, but suddenly his head snapped up, and he felt a cold sinking in his heart—for he knew that he had slept on duty! In the face of deadly peril, the Spider had slept! It made no sense to him, and yet it was a fact. The heaviness of slumber was still in his brain and would not let him think clearly. Something was terribly wrong; something... He tried to swing his legs to the floor and they were leaden weights; without feeling. By the heavens! He had been *drugged!*

With the force of a physical blow, the thought drove Wentworth to his feet. His legs gave way under him, but he struggled up again, braced a rigid arm against the wall while he tried to lift his gun. He concentrated all his attention on lifting the gun and his traitor legs gave way. He stumbled... Why, he was on the floor! Lying flat on the floor! That was what the hard rough pressure against his cheek meant! The Spider set his jaw in fierce determination and—*he heard the door open!*

Wentworth called on the last reserves of his powerful will. The criminals, the attack he had waited, were here! His gun... Wentworth pried his head loose from the floor. With a final wrench of his powerful muscles he lifted his body. He lifted it—one inch! Through a century of effort, he maintained that gain while his titan's will fought for clarity of thought.

Grimly, the Spider realized that his body was helpless; that his brain soon would be the same unless he concentrated all his strength in holding onto consciousness. He had intended to take these men prisoners and force from them the truth concerning this new criminal leader and his weapon of blindness. Now he must rearrange his plans, that was all! He let his body sag limply to the floor.

A man's voice spoke, and there was hard laughter in his tones. "Okay, Joe, you take his feet. There ought to be a Spider outfit around here somewhere. Find it and bring it along. The boss says he'll need it!"

Wentworth heard those words faintly and, within him, he smiled. They would take him to the boss! It was a thought registered in his subconscious, while everything else was blotted out in the white-hot concentration of his will which fought to keep his brain clear. He would not yield to the drug! He *would* not! And presently the boss, these men, would learn what it meant to attack the Master of Men!

# CHAPTER 2
## SLAVES OF DESPAIR

THE DETAILS of being carried from the lodging house to a waiting car, of a jouncing journey across the city, were vague as a half-remembered dream in Wentworth's mind. Yet, through the mighty power of his will, he clung to consciousness. No other man living could have resisted the strength of the drug, but the Spider was a man to whom the impossible was an everyday accomplishment He... *resisted.*

Presently, the effects of the drug began to diminish. He was almost fully conscious when he was carried into a great warehouse and into a hidden elevator which dropped him and his captors swiftly to underground caverns.

Tentatively, he tried the movements of his body. But even his powerful will could not so soon break the tyranny of the anesthetic gas which plainly had been used to overpower him. A dull, persistent throbbing, like the erratic pounding of a laboring heart, began to drum on his ears. The air had the stale stench of oily machines when the elevator door was flung wide and he was thrown roughly upon a stone floor. Powerful hands seized him then, and he felt the cold touch of metal upon wrists and ankles while manacles were snapped home. A man swore and drove his foot violently against Wentworth's ribs.

"The Spider, eh?" he rasped. "The Spider! By God, we'll make him suffer! We'll...."

He gasped, and his voice broke off. He leaped back a full yard and he ripped a gun from a hip holster!

"You try something!" he snarled. "Damn you, Spider, you just try something and I'll fill you with lead!"

Supine upon the floor, chained hand and foot, the Spider could not move. He had merely opened his eyes and looked at the man! But the naked sword-flash of the will behind those eyes had been enough to terrify this armed, powerful criminal!

Wentworth said softly, "What is your name?"

The man who had kicked him was naked to the waist. The gun shook a little in his right fist, and from the left dangled a thick-lashed whip whose ends were tipped with lead. The man laughed raucously to cover his fear.

"Going to remember me, are you, Spider?" the man snarled. "I ain't afraid of you! I'm Mike Bannion! And you'll sweat in Hell under my whip, see?"

A slight smile crossed Wentworth's lips. "Mike Bannion," he murmured.

He turned his eyes away from the man, then glanced about him. A single dim ceiling light threw pale gleams against stone walls that were beaded with moisture. Hunkered down like animals on the floor were four other captive men and two women, and the chains which bound Wentworth's wrists and ankles linked him to them. There were five of the brutal power-ful guards—each with a whip in his fist!

"Up, you punks!" Mike Bannion snarled. "Up on your feet, dogs!"

A whip whined through the air and a man gasped in sudden pain. The whole line surged to its feet, dragging Wentworth upward by the chains that bound him. By an exertion of will, he forced his legs to answer the summons. He could not put added strain upon these poor souls who were prisoners with him.

"Best to obey quietly," he said to them. "They have the power to hurt you… for the present."

The woman ahead of Wentworth seemed too frail for the burden of her chains, and Wentworth moved close to her to ease the strain; caught the grateful, frightened glance of her eyes. The robes of the Spider swung from Wentworth's broad shoulders. In chains, he walked like a king. The thunder of the machines grew mightily as they filed into a narrow corridor and moved onward, accompanied by the jangling of their chains… like ominous music.

Wentworth's eyes were everywhere, probing the secrets of the catacombs. Here were all the trappings of slavery in what was plainly a great underground powerhouse! Great God, who could conceive of a thing like this beneath the crowded metropolitan streets of New York City! Up above, men and women moved about their casual business of work or pleasure, of simple living. Here, beneath the earth, crime festered like a foul growth for the city's ultimate destruction! The Spider had reckoned upon some new rising power; he had found a kingdom of Hell already established!

Fury gnawed at Wentworth's heart, and it was as much anger at himself as at these brutal guards who tortured the unfortunates. He blamed himself that this power had been allowed to wax so strong. The Spider could blame himself, when not all the city's thousands of police had come to suspect this horror! WENTWORTH'S THOUGHTS broke off as a guard

ahead swung open a thick door and the
chained file of prisoners dragged wearily
into a narrow chamber whose longest
wall was a thick pane of glass. When
the door swung shut, the mechanic roar
of the machines was cut off, and lights
built up a glow beyond the glass. Went-
worth gazed narrowly through it into an office outfitted in the
height of luxury and bad taste.

The bloated chairs shrieked with lurid colors and the inch-
es-thick rug cried out against them all in brilliant red. The man
behind the carved mahogany desk had a sagging, fleshy face.
His neck squeezed out above his collar and he twirled a red
rose beneath a blunt nose. His voice came with a thin elegance
through a speaker unit in the glass.

"A poor lot," he said mincingly. "A decidedly poor lot. Best to
kill Number Two at once. She won't last a week."

The woman ahead of Wentworth sagged to her knees. "Oh,
please," she pleaded. "Please! I only look weak! I can work very
hard! I swear I can. I swear…."

A guard's whip whined through the air and Wentworth flung
out an arm, shrouded in his cape; caught the vicious edge of the
blow. Over that sheltering arm, Wentworth's fierce eyes sought
out the eyes of the leader.

"That's twice, Mike Bannion," he said softly.

Bannion's face went pasty white, but before he could speak,
the voice beyond the glass cut in smoothly.

"Ah, yes, and we have with us the chivalrous Spider," he

26

murmured. "If you work well, Spider, I may let you do a few jobs for me up above, too. But you must be very attentive to your duties, Spider, and give proof of your loyalty!"

Wentworth laughed softly, and the sound had a strange carrying power. It cut like the edge of a scimitar swung with a knowing hand.

Beyond the glass, the fat man came sharply to his feet, and his hand was out of sight beneath the edge of the desk. He stood there tautly through a long moment, then came swaggering out toward the glass, as if to prove his courage to himself. That glass was bulletproof, Wentworth saw. The guns of the guards would be of no help to the Spider... yet! The fat man was speaking again. To his own ears, his voice probably seemed smooth, but the loudspeaker picked up its flaws and magnified them. The man's voice was trembling—though he addressed the Spider through bulletproof glass!

"You'll really find me a kind master, Spider," he said "It was twice in my power to have you killed, but I fear you so little I let you live! You are helpless, Spider! You are in chains under the whips and guns of my guards! You do not even know where you are, though that would not matter!"

Wentworth said nothing, but through the glass the mocking coldness of his eyes probed into the master of this Hell. The man licked his lips with a furtive tongue, went on swiftly. His tone became blustering.

"You'll be paid well, all of you. Two and a half cents for each box of a hundred. Sleeping charges are a dollar a night; meals fifty cents. You see, it's easy! A hundred boxes, a mere thousand pieces finished, and you make a day's expenses. Everything else is yours. Of course, there are smaller charges for use of the bath, and the laundry, if you have foolish notions about keeping clean. In these times, you should be glad of the jobs instead of making us chain you up like this!

"Take them away!"

Wentworth's eyes, secret beneath lowered lids, shifted to the guards. A single surging leap would place him beside the nearest and he could snatch a gun! These five whip-torturers richly deserved death at the Spider's hands! His eyes blazed wide and stabbed toward the bellied lump of flesh who was overlord of this Hell beyond the glass, and the man swore in a high, thin voice and scuttled behind his desk.

"Beat him!" he shouted. "Beat him down!"

The guards shifted their feet, one raised his whip… but it did not fall on the Spider. Instead, another man caught the whirling lash… and Wentworth forced himself to calmness. If he provoked a revolt now, these others would suffer more than he. They were sure to be killed in the exchange of bullets. And, until he learned the secret of penetrating this armored room, the man behind the glass was safe. He schooled himself to patience.

"Get moving!" the guards ordered harshly. "Come on, get along there!"

The whips slashed and cracked and the moans of the slaves rose piteously. Only by a violent exertion of will did Wentworth prevent himself from launching at once to the attack. Silently, he swore vengeance for each moment's suffering of these poor prisoners.

"Go ahead," he told the woman beside him gently. "I promise you release… and vengeance! The Spider *swears it!*"

His voice was a whisper, but its dry menace cut through the narrow corridor and stilled even the venom of the guards. In silence then, save for the clank of their dragging chains, the slaves filed back through the thick soundproof door—into the whining, never-ceasing thunder of the machines. Wentworth peered, narrow-eyed. Somewhere there must be an escape.

THE HEAVY rumble of the machines ate into his brain. The damp airless heat weighed physically upon him. Ahead, one of the guards swung wide another door and the mechanical roar of the shop rushed out to meet him, brought with it the stench of hot oil, and of close, superheated air. Then he had gone through the door, behind the woman, and saw the factory itself!

Wentworth had a momentary impression of great spinning wheels mounted on a single shaft that ran the length of the room; of belts that slapped and intertwined as they speared off into dark cubicles to each side of the central aisle. Then, through their mingled whine and roar, he could catch the champing of smaller machines; the regular eccentricity of engines that punched and jarred and grunted until the very stones beneath Wentworth's feet caught up the rhythm and it worked up through the heel bones, through the spine into the very brain. Slowly, the chain of prisoners shuffled forward.

Wentworth's eyes stabbed into the machine alcoves off the main chamber, saw men and women like tortured gnomes in the dim yellow light. One or two lifted dulled eyes, but the rest paid no heed. Only their hands seemed alive. They darted at the work with suppressed fury, as if life itself depended on their speed. Each slave was chained to the iron monster he served, and among them the whip-armed guards kept constant watch!

Wentworth felt his anger burn to white heat at the horror about him. He, who had never known personal fear, felt a mad urge to battle stir within him. No criminal consigned to the galleys of medieval Rome ever faced a fate worse than this!

The blue flame of the blow-torch stabbed toward the guard's face!

These slaves would never see the light of day; never know any fate other than this hopeless, dull racing with time for masters who would never set them free—racing against work that had no beginning and no end, but kept on and on and on....

Patience! Wentworth prompted himself. There was a release, and it must be the Spider who brought it. He could not accomplish it by senseless revolt before the time was ripe. And before he could free these sufferers, he must learn the secrets of this Hell—learn, too, what connection these murderers of souls had with that other horror which had so terribly blinded the police!

From this preoccupation, Wentworth was wrenched by the shriek of a woman. Cry on cry tore from her, and Wentworth saw a half-dozen guards, naked to the waist in the sweltering heat, rush toward the sound with whips swinging in their fists. Wentworth's escort halted the march of the prisoners, and the high whine of the spinning power shaft began to fade; the giant flywheels slowed.

Evil glee shone in Bannion's face as he grinned toward Wentworth and the other prisoners. "This will do you good!" he growled. "You'll see what happens to workers who get ideas!"

The shrieks went on and on....

Wentworth tightened his fists until he could feel the bite of the nails in his palms and his wrist cords swelled against the grip of his manacles. If ever he had heard madness, it was in the screams of that poor tortured woman! His eyes felt hot and strained in his head and he fought against the swift tide of his fury. Stiffly, heavily chained to the six other prisoners, he waited and saw three guards drag the screaming woman from her alcove.

Hard grins were on the faces of the men. Two of them gripped her arms, twisting them up behind her. After them walked the third, and he lightly flicked the biting lead-tipped thongs across her back… a promise of what was to come, but a promise that drew blood! Straight toward the file of prisoners, they dragged the woman—toward the great, main flywheel!

WENTWORTH SWORE harshly under his breath as he grasped the purpose of these sadistic guards. "Bide your time," he had counseled himself, but the Spider's great heart would not permit him to stand idly by while this poor woman was tortured to death! Yet how, in the name of heaven, could the Spider, without weapons and encumbered by the chains that bound him to six other helpless victims, hope to do anything?

Wentworth's jaw jutted strongly and a cold calm settled on his brain. It was not a question of what was possible. He must save her! Wentworth's eyes darted about with cool calculation. Not three yards from where he stood, one of the guards had set down a blowtorch. A jagged tail of blue flame still guttered from its nozzle and, eyeing it, Wentworth felt his lips draw thin against his teeth. He had found his weapon!

Straight toward the flywheel the guards dragged the girl. Golden hair swung limply about her face, and there were the dark smudges of shadows beneath eyes that no longer held human intelligence. Still her cheeks puffed, her lips stretched with the pressure of the bottled screams that were tearing from her very heart! She made no resistance to the guards who wrenched her along by her twisted arms. It was as if that scream had no tangible connection with her brutalized body; as if her soul already had detached itself from torment.

It was only when she confronted the flywheel that she seemed to understand the thing that threatened. She began to fight then, wrenching furiously against the grip of the guards, so that men of Wentworth's own escort bounded laughingly forward to assist in subduing that lone woman!

They lifted her bodily from the floor, stretched arms and legs to the great, thick spokes of the wheel and bound them there, ripped off her clothing with rough hands. Even before that task was finished, a gnout whistled through the air to lay its streaks of torn red across her white body! It was Mike Bannion who ran toward a switch upon the wall. The other guards drew back, poising their whips!

"Bet I catch her more times than you, Bill," one jeered at another. "The drinks are on me if you win!"

The other guard laughed hoarsely. "Remember that last one! Had a Hell of a time finding how many hit her. Wasn't nothing but whip-cuts!"

Dazed, the girl hung now upon the flywheel. The strain of the ropes corded the ligaments of her frail body almost to breaking. In a moment that great flywheel would begin to revolve, to spin upon the power shaft. When the half-dozen whips whirled to catch her speeding body....

Wentworth had edged halfway toward the flame-spitting torch. The chains that bound him to the woman ahead, and to the man behind, were stretched taut. They did not notice his action—and neither did the guard. All eyes, fearful or gloating, were fixed upon that strained and tortured body bound on the wheel. As Bannion reached toward the switch that would throw power into the shaft and set that titanic torture wheel to spinning, Wentworth gathered his strength—and hurled himself toward the blowtorch!

There was a strangled shout from the prisoner behind Wentworth, as the chains yanked taut. The woman ahead of him spilled limply to the ground with the violence of his charge—but the Spider's hands closed upon the blowtorch! Wrestling against the drag of his chains, he thrust the torch straight before him! His hand spun the supply valve and with a hissing of released air, the blue flame licked straight at the brutal face of Bannion!

Mike Bannion whirled at the shouts, and his whip was drawn back to strike. Even as the flame stabbed toward him, the gnout whistled through the air and its multiple thongs bit into Wentworth's face and throat!

"That's three times, Bannion!" Wentworth cried—and then, the Spider laughed! The sound was bitter and mocking as death itself. He laughed, and strength flowed through him. He walked steadily forward, pulling the entire file of struggling prisoners with him, thrusting flame before him like a sword!

For a single instant, Bannion stood against the torment of the flame and he clawed out his gun! But with the weapon already in his fist, he shrieked and threw his arms high in agony and turned to run! The blue flame splashed across his shoulder and wrapped for an instant lovingly about his skull. His hair vanished in a crisping flash, Bannion pitched forward, screaming, to the floor! His whip lay where it had dropped from his clawing hand, and Wentworth caught it up eagerly… but the revolver had been flung a score of feet away!

Suddenly, the other guards were upon the Spider! Biting, stinging leather thongs ate into his shoulders, cut across his head, wrapped about his throat. He whirled, and flame struck out toward the men. He tried to swing the whip, but the chains held him in check, snatched at ankles and wrists. Through the bedlam of shouts and curses that lifted around him, he heard another fearsome sound—the mounting whine as the flywheel gathered speed!

In despair, Wentworth realized that he has not reached the man in time to prevent his throwing the switch. He heard the girl's voice lift to a high shriek, a guttering, shuddering cry under the centrifugal fury of the wheel. He stabbed flame toward the face of a guard, sent the man screaming backward; lashed another across the chest with the blue sword of the blowtorch. They shrank back, but there were others behind him whose whips ate and ate at his flesh. The clothing was shredded from his body. The prostrate captives, chained to him, were a dead weight he could not move.

He twisted the flame against the men behind him, and they leaped back, but others were upon him again with their destroying flails. Twice, three times, Wentworth stabbed out with the flame, to drive men back. He could not reach the switch. With a final, fierce wrench, he brought the blowtorch to focus on the insulation of the wires.

He had won!

There was a blinding flash of light that drove him backward the full length of his chains. They tripped him, slammed him down on his face, and the torch flew from his hands. Instantly, the guards were upon him like a worrying pack of dogs. The whips rose and fell, rose and fell. They drank deep. Long after consciousness left his body, the gnouts continued to drink....

But the huge flywheel, with its human freight, had stopped!

## CHAPTER 3
## THE SPIDER'S
## FIGHTING MATE

TO NITA VAN SLOAN, life had become a very empty thing. Surrounded by those who had loved and served Richard Wentworth so faithfully before he was forced into hiding, she had only one thought—to help the man she loved. But she could not do that—because Nita did not even know in what disguise Wentworth hid from his many enemies, nor where he had secreted himself!

Worry had thinned the sweet oval of Nita's face, and laid dark shadows beneath her eyes. She knew that the police kept a ceaseless watch over her activities, trying to snare Dick. It was not that, however, which kept him from her side. Rather it was his chivalry that would not permit him to involve her in the perilous pattern of his own existence! So it was that only occasionally, and then through the newspapers, she received some hint of Dick's activities. It was the only proof she had that he still lived!

Now the headlines were blazoning forth the lie that the Spider, trapped in a common safe robbery, had released some unknown gas which had put out the eyes of fourteen policemen!

Indignation at that blaspheming falsehood made the news sheets rustle in Nita's shaking hands, yet there was little she could do to stop this defamation, unless… unless she could trap the criminal who really was guilty! So, she might cross Dick's trail—might once more know, if only for brief moments, the sheltering love of his arms!

She sent the two men who served and loved the Spider—the burly Sikh, Ram Singh, and the stalwart Jackson—to forage for information in the underworld. Within the hour, Ronald Jackson returned to Nita's Fifth Avenue apartment and there was a burning deep anger in his eyes… yet his voice was different.

"Miss Nita," he said heavily, "it's bad news I bring you."

Nita came slowly to her feet, but her violet eyes were steady despite the pallor of her cheeks.

"Yes, Jackson," she said quietly and waited.

Jackson's hands drew into heavy fists. "I know you can take it, Miss Nita," he said slowly, "but it's so little. Nothing to work on."

"Out with it, Jackson," Nita ordered crisply, and Jackson stiffened, like the soldier he had been, under the voice of authority. His voice became formal, stereotyped.

"According to orders," he said, "I proceeded to four different crook hangouts and kept my ears open. I heard the same thing in all four places, and…."

He hesitated and Nita moved a hand impatiently. "Am I a child, Jackson?" she demanded. "He isn't... Master Dick isn't...."

"Dead? No, Miss Nita, not that." Jackson rolled his shoulders as if he picked up a burden. "There's a new power in the underworld, Miss Nita, whose name nobody says, but the grapevine has it... Master Dick is his prisoner!"

Nita's breath came out in a sigh. It was heavy news, and perilous for Dick, but from his manner... Nita felt her heart lift. Many men before this had tried to hold the Spider prisoner!

"Good," she acknowledged crisply. "Now, find me the name of this underworld leader, and his hideout. Then we can act!"

Nita's hopes were high, but that first slim budget of information was all that she could learn through a week of fierce effort. Then came the old news of the note that had been left by the Spider in Lauder's safe—a fact which police had not revealed to the newspapers. It seemed to have no importance, but somehow she must use the little she had learned. There was nothing else, though three times during the week banks had been robbed and, in each case, defending policemen had been blinded! The newspaper shouted for the capture and punishment of the Spider.

So it was that on the eighth day after she had begun the search—and it was eighth, too, of the Spider's imprisonment—Nita called Ram Singh and Jackson to the library where she paced tautly back and forth. The deep violet of her eyes blazed against the pallor of her face and the eyes of the two men followed her every movement—Ram Singh with arms folded across his broad chest where he stood beside the door; Jackson at the window, as sharply at attention as though on parade.

NITA'S WORDS came out jerkily, and there was a roughness in her usually soft, deep voice. "We know so little," she said. "It is useless to attempt to solve these robberies. The police are working on them with all their resources. We do not know that Master Dick was seized because of his threats to Lauder…."

Ram Singh's voice rumbled out through his bristling black beard. "*Wah!* It is not difficult to find out! Jackson and I, we will take this Lauder and question him in a way I know of!" His hand dropped to the brass hilt of a great knife in his sash. "I think that he will speak true words!"

" 'Twouldn't do," Jackson said shortly, and the glare of Ram Singh's eyes swung toward him.

"It is a soldier's plan, Jackson *sahib,*" Ram Singh softened his nasal voice to a rumble. "But it is well known thou art only an imitation of a soldier, and…."

"Peace," Nita interrupted the two bridling men, and there was a wan smile on her lips. Quarrel they must, since it was their way, but each had risked his life for the other a score of times. If there were only something positive to fight, instead of this fishing—for shadows!

"Ram Singh's plan we may have to try," she went on quietly, "but first we would have to make sure that Lauder was guilty. The master would not tolerate injury to an innocent person!"

"I will trail him night and day," Jackson volunteered. "It would be better if there were two of us, but this great bearded fool, who cannot shed his turban, would be spotted at once."

"Now, by Kali!" Ram Singh ripped out. "In a dark room, with knives...."

"Are you men or children?" Nita demanded scornfully. "The master is in danger, and you quibble with your petty jealousies. You may go. I will handle this matter alone!"

"Now, Miss Nita...."

*"Wah, missie sahib,* this tin soldier..." Ram Singh checked and salaamed, lifting cupped hands to his forehead. "Speak! We hear and obey! And if this beardless fool gets stubborn...."

Jackson's big fists knotted. "Just give your orders, Miss Nita, and I'll make the heathen toe the mark."

Nita smiled into the fierce loyalty of their gaze. "These are my orders," she said quietly. "You will go into the underworld in whatever guise you think best, and try there to find some clue to the identity or whereabouts of this 'Big Guy,' as they call him. I will handle Lauder."

Protests leaped to the lips of the two men, but Nita's eyes grew chill, and there was in her voice a trace of the crisp accent of Richard Wentworth when she spoke. "It is an order!"

The two men saluted after their kind, Ram Singh salaaming low with his muttered formula, "I hear and obey, *missie sahib!*"

Jackson saluted, pivoted in a right-about, and marched from the room. In the hallway, their voices lifted again in sharp debate....

Nita sank upon a window seat where warm sunlight streamed, bringing the glitter of the distant East River. Her narrow white hands twisted together. It was so hard now that Dick's reassuring strength was withdrawn. She closed her eyes and tried to reach out to him with her mind, with her soul, as so often she had done before in moments of stress. Peace would not come, only the increasing, fearful sense of peril... and Nita sprang to her feet with her hands pressed hard against her lips. Oh, it was true, the thing Jackson had learned! Dick was in awful danger....

Nita's eyes swung wildly about the subdued beauty of her library, scarcely saw old Jenkyns, the butler, beside the door, tea

"So!" Amoy grunted.

"The show commences!"

tray in his hands. He came forward quietly, and there was worry, too, on his wrinkled face. It seemed to Nita that it was less ruddy than usual beneath the crisp silver cap of his hair. Jenkyns, too, felt the strain of separation from his beloved Master Richie, whose father before him he had served.

"I worry, Miss Nita," he acknowledged when Nita questioned him. "No use saying I don't, but it's a little silly in a man my age. I should have learned better. Master Richie has a way of coming through. I feel a little wicked, believing in him so, but Miss Nita, sometime I doubt even death itself, God forgive me, can ever stop him from… coming through. More especially if somebody needs him. If you need him…."

Nita's eyes clung to Jenkyns' wrinkled, kindly face and slowly the doubts and the fears faded from her mind. "Thank you, Jenkyns," she said gently. "I feel ashamed that my faith is less than yours!"

Thereafter, she laid her own plans swiftly. A phone call would just catch John Lauder at his office. Probably too late to see him today, unless….

"It's rather urgent, Mr. Lauder," Nita said when she got through to the lawyer. "It isn't anything that I can talk about over the telephone. As a matter of fact, I'm not sure the wire isn't tapped, but I feel it's important to see you at once."

Lauder's voice was suave. "For such clients as you, Miss van Sloan," he said, "my office hours never end. Would it be presumptuous of me to suggest dinner? My car could call for you in an hour."

Nita assented with a secret sharpening of her eyes. Lauder

seemed almost too eager! He must be fully aware of her connection with Dick, and of the charges that too often had linked Dick with the operations of the Spider. Almost, she was tempted to order Ram Singh to follow her. But surely she could handle Lauder! Nevertheless, before she left, she gave implicit directions to Jenkyns and, beneath the silken sash that she bound loosely about the flowing dull blue silk of her dress, she secured a small automatic. It fitted close against her body in a special holster Dick had made for her, and her dress did not sag with its weight.

NITA WAS not sure exactly what she hoped to learn from Lauder. It would be a matter of convincing herself whether he was actively engaged in warfare against the Spider. Her own story to him was simple. She expected, she said, to be charged with assisting Richard Wentworth to hide from the police, and she wanted a lawyer. "The best," she smiled frankly into Lauder's eyes across the secluded table in the dinner club Lauder had chosen. "After what you did for Frank Rocker, I felt sure you could handle such a simple case as mine."

Lauder dropped his eyes to where one carefully manicured hand toyed with a wine glass, and it seemed to Nita that a cautious veil had been drawn over his suave pink-and-white face.

"It is well," Lauder said slowly, "to know the full dangers to a client—that is, the truth." His careful smile showed just the edges of his even white teeth, and did not disturb the waxed mustache. "Have you... hidden... Mr. Wentworth?"

"I have neither seen him, nor had word from him in three months," Nita said steadily, though the truth was an ache in her heart. "He is afraid of involving me, and consequently stays away."

Lauder's eyes held a falsely merry light. "He shows admirable restraint! But I do not, then, see what worries you about the police."

Nita met his eyes with a pretty air of confiding. "You will say I am foolish," she acknowledged, "but for over a week I have been terribly worried… about nothing."

"Intuition?" Lauder was not looking at her, but beyond her, and Nita saw his eyes widen with a suggestion of surprise… or it might be fear! Her hands, twisted in her lap, pressed against the automatic under her sash.

"I'm afraid," Lauder said softly, "that we are going to be interrupted!"

The shadow of a man fell across the table, a grossly fat man, and his voice came with a delicate precision. "Ah, Mr. Lauder! Quite a coincidence!" A hand rested on the white cloth, and the knuckles were soft and dimpled. The sparse long black hairs upon its back seemed alive. Nita repressed a shudder with difficulty.

Lauder's close-shaven jaw showed small indentations from the hard compression of muscles. "I cannot discuss business here," he said curtly.

The fat man laughed with an effect of panting. "Certainly not, Mr. Lauder—not here! But at my home, yes! You will come… and the young lady. I could not bear to think of interrupting a social evening. At my home, yes." His enunciation was offensively exact.

Nita lifted her gaze to the man's face, but the beady eyes were focused on Lauder, and the folds of round, smoothly pink cheeks hid them from her. She was aware that another man stood behind her chair, and a third circled toward Lauder. Nita's breath came more quickly. Her hand compressed the butt of her automatic. Was all this planned? Lauder had selected the dinner club; the arrival of these men was pat. But there was a grayness beneath the even ruddiness of Lauder's face! He lurched to his feet awkwardly, and his eyes darted about like small frightened mice.

"You threaten me?" he asked hoarsely.

The fat man lifted his dimpled hand from the table in a deprecating gesture. "Surely, that is unnecessary, my dear Lauder," the man was still laughing. "I invite you to take a small trip to my home, where I shall lay a certain proposition before you—with inducements. I took the liberty of settling your check." He turned his shoulder on Lauder, and it involved a heavy movement of his whole padded body. His bow to Nita did not make his formal shirtfront buckle, nor disturb the rosebud on his lapel. "May I assist you with your wrap, madame?"

For the first time, Nita met the fat man's eyes, and they were merry and mocking, black flakes of obsidian between sly wrinkles of fat. They crawled over the graceful décolletage of Nita's gown. His outstretched palm was moist.

Somehow, Nita put a smile on her full red lips, and hid her racing thoughts behind a widening of violet eyes. She had come to learn Lauder's possible connection with the capture of Richard Wentworth, hadn't she? Yet she wished she had bidden Ram Singh to follow her!

"Why, I think that would be pleasant!" she cried, "but it is for Mr. Lauder to say."

Lauder apparently was beyond words. The third man had moved to his side, and a hand was thrust deep into a coat pocket that held more than a fist. Nita's wrap settled about her shoulders, and the passage across the dinner club was inconspicuous. The fat man moved beside her with a tread that was not audible, and his voice wheezed out pleasantries. Nita forced a small laugh and tried to draw comfort from the weight of the automatic beneath her sash. She found herself wondering whether a bullet would penetrate so much fat. She shivered a little.

"You are cold, madame?" came the fat man's voice, gently. "It is a thing we must remedy!"

THE LIMOUSINE into which she was ushered was tightly closed, and held a scented heat that was suffocating. The windows had seemed ordinary, but once Nita was inside, she could see nothing at all of the streets!

"Really very simple," the fat man murmured in her ear. "One likes privacy, and Polaroid glass, installed so that the refraction of two sheets falls at right angles, effectively shuts off all vision."

"Oh, and is this glass bulletproof, too?" Nita asked.

The man's moist palm patted her arm familiarly. "You are clever, madame," he said. "Very clever. Yet I think no one will shoot at us. I think no one will follow us… not for long!"

John Lauder sat as stiffly upright as a waxen figure. If his fear was assumed, it was cleverly put on. Nita comforted herself that surely this was leading her closer to Dick; she hoped frantically that it did! Small talk became a strain, then a labor, but she continued her pretense of ignorance. Presently the car slid smoothly to a halt and, ushered from the car, Nita had a brief glimpse of concrete walls before she entered an elevator whose sides were hung with gaudy silks. They fluttered slightly in the draft of motion, parted to reveal a violently colorful room with a crimson carpet.

Lauder burst his silence. "Confound it, Amoy!" he said harshly. "There is no sense to this. I told you flatly that I couldn't handle your business, and…."

"So, I invite you to see others who did not wish to work for me," the fat man wheezed. "I have arranged a little show of these people who did not wish to work for me. Afterward, I shall give you your choice. So!"

The chair into which Nita was thrust seemed to absorb her and drain her of all bodily strength., Air hissed softly from the seams of the leather. Nita controlled a shudder of revulsion. It was like sitting on an incredibly fat man. Impossible to rise swiftly from this chair. The gun against her side seemed a puny trifle. The fat man, Amoy, bent over her with his small, sly eyes, and his hand struck like a snake to snatch Nita's concealed automatic.

"There is no need for this… among *friends,*" he chuckled.

Nita smiled, and lifted a rounded shoulder against the dull blue of her gown. "Of course not," she agreed lightly. "Why didn't you say you were interested?"

"So," Amoy grunted, and heaved himself into a thick chair behind the desk. "So, the show commences!"

At the touch of a button on his desk, silks that hid the walls parted to reveal a long pane of glass. Lights illuminated brilliantly the narrow concrete corridor beyond. A door opened, and a man stepped heavily through the aperture. Behind him, another man, stripped to the waist and with a brutal whip in his fist, stood at ease.

"Get down on your knees," Amoy whispered into an annunciator, and the captive plumped down with a fearful glance at the whip. "You will worship at the shrine," Amoy purred, and the man bumped his forehead on the concrete floor. Amoy reached for the rose in a vase on his desk. Lauder was bent tensely forward in his chair.

"I see, Lauder, that you recognize this man," Amoy chuckled. "You are right; he is Frank Rocker. Somewhat notorious as a killer, I believe. Not a man to take humiliation calmly, eh Lauder? Yet he… *worships at the shrine!*"

Nita shivered. There was blood on the forehead of Frank Rocker, yet he continued, fearfully, to bump the concrete floor. Nita felt a hard, slow throbbing of her heart. She set her teeth on her lip, and fought against the panic horror of thoughts that she would not recognize. The thing she feared could not be; it could not! *Dick…* Amoy's chuckle rasped on her flesh like a file. There was now another man beside Rocker, bumping his forehead also, and she heard Amoy's explanation of his identity, faintly. There was a swimming before her eyes, and blackness in her brain.

"A very famous detective," Amoy was saying. "I believe they

called him the ace of the homicide department. Henry Kade. He is wanted now for the murder of a man he was supposed to protect. Some two hundred and fifty thousand dollars in jewels was stolen from that man. *Kade* didn't profit by it; *he* didn't commit the murder! But Kade would commit a murder now, if I ordered him to, wouldn't you, Kade?"

Kade bumped his forehead frenziedly on the floor. "Whatever you order, master!" he cried.

"You see, Lauder," Amoy said gently. "Men work for me when I wish it, regardless of their personal desires. Will you handle my business, Lauder?"

Lauder tried to struggle to his feet, but one of Amoy's two guards struck the back of his hand across Lauder's face. Lauder slumped into the chair and a thread of blood seeped from his mouth corner. His waxed mustache was limp.

"One way or another," Amoy whispered. "Men obey me! I have another little exhibit, Lauder. A while ago you were threatened, and my protection extends even to those whom I have chosen to serve me... against their will! I have... protected you, Lauder. So!"

ANOTHER MAN staggered through the doorway where the guard with the whip stood, and there were chains upon his wrists and upon his ankles. There was a red, unhealed whip-welt across his unshaven face, black with a week's beard, and he carried himself in evident pain. When the brutal thrust of a guard sent him to his knees, his back was a crisscrossed mass of whip cuts....

Nita thrust both hands to her mouth, but she could not quite strangle the cry that rose to her quivering lips. Blackness reeled before her eyes, and Amoy's hateful voice thrust needles of pain into her heart.

"Ah, I see that you already recognize Exhibit Three. My dear Lauder, allow me to present... *The Spider!*"

Nita forced the faintness from her brain and her eyes reached out to where Dick—her Dick—knelt on the concrete floor of that walled-off corridor. So pitifully beaten, so helpless in his chains and wounds. Her lips grew firm, and she gathered her strength and will. There were guns in this room, and Dick... She peered toward him, and his head lifted for an instant. Nita almost cried aloud in joy. His eyes recognized her, and she caught the naked power of his will in them as clearly as if he whispered in her ear....

"Wait!" those eyes told her. *"Wait! The time is not yet!"*

Nita bowed her head in humbleness and the tears of thanksgiving formed in her eyes. Wounded the Spider might be; wounded in body and soul, but the man who could master and subdue him had not yet been born! If he bowed now in seeming humbleness before this pig of a man, it was because it served his own purposes. *The time was not yet....*

"The Spider was stubborn," Amoy's hateful voice was purring, "but he, too, has yielded to my will in the space of one short week, Lauder. Do you think you could hold out so long, Lauder?"

Lauder jerked to his feet. His voice was strangled. "God, let me out of here!"

"Yes," said Amoy. "You will handle my business. The pay will be excellent even for your high standards. Fail me, and I will reduce you to slavery. For men serve me, if I wish! Ah yes, Lauder… and the young lady will remain as hostage for your good behavior! I have no idea that your affections are involved, but it is known that she went out with you this evening, and her disappearance might be called kidnapping and murder—if I wish. That will depend on how you serve me, Lauder!"

Lauder was leaning heavily on the desk of Amoy, all his body sagging. He pushed off and began to stagger aimlessly about the room, and his voice was a bleat of anguish. "Let me out—oh, let me out! God, yes, Amoy. Whatever you say…."

But Nita's tear-dimmed eyes were there in the corridor where, under the threatening lash of the guard, Dick knelt on the floor. She had recoiled from the course that duty had thrust upon her, yet Dick could bend his pride and will to this humility so that he might serve the people and triumph in the end! Once more, her eyes reached out to his, and there was a smile in the blue-gray gaze of the Spider!

Nita made no sound at all. Rigid as stone she sat in her chair; cold as stone, too, was her heart in her breast and as heavy. Dick's courage she could not doubt, nor his strength… but Amoy was *so sure!* And this awful hole in the earth, these whip-armed guards… In the corridor, the Spider still knelt motionless on the concrete floor. Nita's head sagged forward into her lifted hands. It was only then that the silken curtains fell to cut out that awful vision….

AT THE rasp of the whip-guard's order, Wentworth dragged his chains upward. With the others, he made his wooden way back through the soundproofed door toward the beat and hot

stink of the machinery. The heaviness in Wentworth's movements had nothing to do with pain or weariness or despair. He
must move deliberately lest his fury burst from the iron disci-
pline of his will! He must not strike before it was time, but, great
God… Nita in this Hell! Nita in the fat hands of Amoy!

Wentworth moved obediently back to his alcove, and a chain
that fastened his ankle to the machine was locked fast. With
simulated dullness he looked about him and set his hands to
work upon the machine, which stuffed a long row of cartridges
with smokeless powder. Chained beside him, working at another
part of the machine, was the homicide detective, Henry Kade.
Wentworth had been feigning a stupor of pain throughout the
long week he had been here, for he could not know whether to
trust Kade. Since he knew the truth, that Kade had been framed
by Amoy, there was no longer need for that caution. He turned
his keen blue-gray eyes on Kade, and saw the man's surprise.

"You're Henry Kade," Wentworth said quietly. "You were on
homicide under Kirkpatrick."

Kade nodded, and the direct gray gaze of his eyes met
Wentworth's. "You're the Spider," he said. "I've chased you and
admired you through a number of years. I swapped lead with
you once, and afterward realized you were only shooting at the
light over my head, and not at me. You're a strange and secret
man, Spider. I've been trying to figure out who you are, but those
whip cuts across your face, and that beard… Even if I ever get
back on the force again, I couldn't put a name to you." He broke
off. "Get to work. Guard coming. Be careful. You've been out
on your feet for a week!"

## THE SPIDER AND THE EYELESS LEGION

Wentworth turned swiftly back to his task and knew that his subterfuge of the last week had succeeded since even Kade, who shared his cell, had been deceived! So much submissiveness had been necessary because he had so terrified the guards at the beginning. Now he must soothe their fears so that they would relax their watch—and then the Spider would lead these slaves of Hell in rebellion!

Slowly, Wentworth canvassed the details of the plan he had been building in his mind. There was no escape from the narrow cells, barely wide enough for the two plank beds, one above another. They had gratings of tool steel, and block locks. No escape either from the long, heavy chain to which each worker in turn was locked morning and evening for the march from cells to machines. The leg irons were always secured either in the cell or at the machine before another lock freed them from the chain....

A guard walked heavily past the alcove opening, whip greedily ready in his hands, and Wentworth bent more attentively over his machine while fires burned coldly in his eyes. But he had found a way—now that he was sure Kade could be relied upon for help!

When the heavy dragging of the prisoner-chain stopped at the entrance of Wentworth's machine alcove that night, he submitted once more to the locking of the ankle irons. With the rest, he and Kade tramped back to their cell, heard the heavy door clang shut and lock. Food was shoved in at the gratings of their cells, but as Kade snatched for it, Wentworth thrust him curtly back.

"There are drugs in that food," he said quietly. "It's used to keep our minds dead."

Kade eyed him sharply. "So that's why you haven't been eating at night all this week! You were faking this business of being out on your feet, and... By God, I believe you're right about the drugs! Many nights I've planned to lie awake and figure a way out. But always, I fell off asleep. It must be in the night food!"

"We'll have to pretend to eat," Wentworth said crisply. It was torture to scrape off the food into the bucket that served as a sanitary arrangement, but it had to be done. He did it quickly, lest the temptation be too great. God knew, they did not over-feed their slaves! Outside, in the corridor, a woman began to scream curses, and a whip sang through the air. Kade peered out of the grating.

"It's the girl Amoy has sent for every night," he said. "He kept putting her on tougher and tougher machines; kept her at it longer hours, with a guard to whip her if she slowed up. She... gave in. She hasn't been out of his quarters for two weeks."

"But tonight, he's sending her back?" Wentworth asked slowly.

Kade's projected head, a dark blur against the ceiling which a dim corridor light illumined, nodded slightly. "He always does, after a while, and then..." His voice bit off.

"What's up?" Wentworth pressed close against the grating.

"Don't look," Kade urged sharply. "It won't help."

Wentworth ignored him, and peered out into the corridor. Two guards were striding past the cell, each with his hand clamped on a girl's arm—a girl who carried her head proudly, who walked with a white, set horror upon her face, and looked to neither side. She was Nita Van Sloan.

Wentworth's hands locked on the steel grating, and the muscles ridged in his forearms. Tonight, Amoy was sending for another girl... for Nita!

Wentworth bit down the fury that burned at his lips. Instead he whispered softly into the darkness.

"Courage," he whispered. "Have courage!"

He saw Nita control her start, as the angry eyes of the guards swept the gratings... But Wentworth had time to see a new strength straighten Nita's back. He heard her laughter, deep and sweet in this vile hole. Then she was gone. Down the corridor, the other girl's screamed curses rose more shrilly, until a whip whined, and the curses broke into screams, and then became broken, dry sobbing.

Wentworth sank back upon his plank bed, and sat staring blindly at the yellow, steel-striped square of the grating until presently even that went dark, and there was no light at all. Sounds blotted out, one by one; the snores of the drugged slaves were like moans. Finally, Nita came back, and her feet dragged, and a whip whined once before her cell door clanged shut—too far away for Wentworth's voice to reach.

Out of the darkness, Wentworth spoke, his voice harshly thin, "Kade, can you do two men's work for two days?"

Kade's voice was disembodied, hollow. He spoke against the ceiling. "I can. You have a plan?"

Wentworth choked down the irony of his laughter. "Call it

madness," he said. "Still, in two days, I believe I can fix the locks on our machine-irons so they will only appear to lock!"

Kade said, doubtfully, "That's a first step, of course. But without weapons; with all the rest of the prisoners chained up, or too frightened to breathe above a whisper? What can we do?"

Wentworth said grimly, "For that, too, I have a madness to offer! But one thing at a time. First, the locks on the machine chains, and then…."

Kade's hand groped down through the darkness and Wentworth somehow sensed it, lifted his own to meet the solid grip.

"We have been on opposite sides of the law, Spider," Kade said softly. "I won't say that we won't be again, if I ever get free of this and clear the frame-up against me. But until that time, I'll say this: I know no man I'd rather follow. I know of no other man who could give me hope!"

Wentworth clasped Kade's hand tightly. "I may lead you only to death," he said curtly, "but it will be a man's death!"

Kade laughed, and the sound was hard and dry as a sob. "A man!" he said. "Spider, you remind me of something I had almost forgotten. We are… *men!*"

## CHAPTER 4
## REBELLION IN HELL

WENTWORTH DARED not even whisper to Kade the nature of his plans for release from his underground Hell, lest there be spies nearby to overhear. Even a whisper was suspicious in this drug-slumbering catacomb. Long after Kade's deep regular breathing announced that he slept, Wentworth lay with burning eyes staring into the darkness of his cell. He was forced to lie on a side, with an arm doubled beneath his head, because of the cruelty of the hard plank against his lacerated back. The place crawled with vermin, and the stench of the buckets, of men long unwashed and drenched with the sweat of this suffocating pit, was a nauseous thing. And Wentworth dared not think of Nita and what she had suffered.

The hot yellow dawn of the hellhole began when the lights flared in the corridors and the guards strode past the gratings, cursing, rattling whip handles across the bars... and shoving in the poor plate of thin gruel that was breakfast. Wentworth crawled from his hard plank to squeeze his body into the narrow opening between bunk and door—the only place where it was possible to stand between the in-crowding walls. Kade slipped down to stand beside him, and they levered the planks upward on their chains, and thereafter had a space three feet by seven in which to move about.

"This should be safe," Wentworth muttered with unmoving lips as he passed the gruel to Kade. "Remember, we are supposed to be drugged! Stumble, and move sluggishly."

They appeared to be spiritless automatons when the cell door clanged open and the ready whips of the guards flicked them into line, to be locked to the heavy prisoner-chain by anklets. Wentworth's uncombed head sagged forward and his cheeks bristled with a dense, black beard. His sole clothing was a pair of filthy trousers and his feet were bare. He looked exactly like all these other men. The women fared scarcely better, for their clothing consisted of a formless slip of sackcloth. Just ahead of Wentworth was the girl who, last night, had been brought back from the quarters of Amoy. Her golden hair hung smoothly about her shoulders, and she carried her head with defiance. The drugs had not begun to work on her again. Nita was far down the chain behind him, and he dared not look that way lest he make things more difficult for her.

Heavily, the line of prisoners shuffled toward the workshop, dragging the hundredweights of chain with bowed shoulders and scuffling feet. They stopped by a machine like a huge mixing bowl. Ahead of Wentworth, the guard jerked a chain riveted to the machine, and clamped the other end about the ankle of the blonde girl. She looked up, startled.

"Hey, this ain't my machine. Hey… Oh, God, not this one! *Not this!*"

She began to beat at the stooping guard with her fists. Her hand darted to the automatic that swung at the man's hip, jerked it free! Before she could even thumb off the safety, a half-dozen whips were driving her to her knees.

"Oh, please, not this machine! Please! *It will put out my eyes!*"

Wentworth's gaze tightened at the echo of the words. He was allowing himself to be chained to the bullet machine with Kade… He knew now the purpose of this sweatshop! Here they made the bullets that had blinded the police.

How they had been used on the night of his own capture he could not guess, but he was sure of his premise. What a fearsome weapon! With its help, the criminals could strike at will and be safe from the police; for any man who attacked them would be blinded!

Something of this he whispered to Kade while his hands flew about his task, waiting until the morning patrol of the guards was finished. Kade stared at him curiously, but made no comment. It was only much later that Wentworth realized Kade had, like the rest of the city, attributed the blinding of the police to their combat with the Spider!

The champing of the machine seemed to bite into his nerves with each passing minute until it seemed he must scream as the only possible release. It was not until he noticed a twitch in Kade's left eye, and involuntary shudders that ran through his body, that he realized the awful truth!

"My God, Kade," he whispered. "There must be drugs in the other food, too! We've been turned into drug addicts!"

Wentworth stared before him with unseeing eyes, and only the hissed warning from Kade's lips that a guard was approaching made him bend to his work in time. Now, they had no choice; now they must eat at least a portion of the drugged food lest their own tormented bodies betray to their captors that they had avoided the narcotics which kept them servile to the slave masters!

It was an hour before Wentworth could turn over the entire operation of the machine to the quivering Kade, and set to work upon the lock on his ankle. It was a delicate task that faced him. He must pick the lock, take it apart and file down the catch. It would not do to jam it. He must shape the dog so that when the anklet was snapped upon him tomorrow morning, it would seem to fasten itself… yet leave it so that actually he could free himself in a brief while! Tomorrow, he must do the same for Kade's chains. Then when, tomorrow night, the guard came to lock them to the prison-chain, they would be free to leap upon him and overpower him. His gun and whip; his keys….

THROUGHOUT THE long day, Wentworth labored over the obdurate metal, and Kade worked the machine alone and hissed warning when the guards were coming. At night, their narcotic-starved nerves were almost beyond control. Only by straining their chains tightly against their bodies could they stop the trembling of their hands and the jerking of their shoulders; only by bowing their heads as if with weariness could they conceal the betraying grimaces. And there was a quivering eagerness as they snatched for their plates of food that night.

"Easy," Wentworth warned, despite the gnawing in his belly, the hard clench of his hands upon the platter of foul food. "Just a little to calm our nerves; and save a bit for tomorrow. We cannot afford to let it dull our brains."

But it didn't work.

Kade snarled amid his bristling beard, and clutched the tin plate against his chest. He backed away from Wentworth the length of the cell.

He was wild-eyed.

"You want to steal it for yourself," he rasped. "Take a step toward me and I'll strangle you!"

He began to wolf the contents of the plate, but his eyes remained burning upon Wentworth's face. Wentworth's body was jerking uncontrollably, but he set his platter down. His leap was without a moment's warning, and his fists struck in perfect timing—but his body was weak. The platter spilled to the floor between them, and Kade's hands flashed out to lock about Wentworth's throat! He bore Wentworth backward to the floor!

Was this the end?

Wentworth lifted a trembling right hand and set it beneath Kade's chin, stiffened his arm. Stubbornly, the muscles of Kade's neck set themselves in resistance, and with his last gasp of strength, Wentworth drove stiffened fingers between the rigid throat-cords, and found the nerve center he sought. Kade slumped across his chest, and for long moments Wentworth lay, unable to stir beneath the weight.

Faintness….

Finally, his head cleared and he could roll Kade's body aside and scrape up the spilled food. He set the two platters upon the floor and crouched beside them, waiting. Horror and hunger crawled in his belly. In God's name, what hope was there for them, while this madness worked on their brains? Wentworth set his jaw. He was the Spider! He would find the way! If they escaped, it was possible they could destroy the criminal who was uniting the underworld behind his fearsome weapon that destroyed the eyes of the law. It was possible… And the Spider was accustomed to accomplish the impossible!

Wentworth's jaw locked so that his teeth ached with the pressure and, even so, the grimaces of his gnawing hunger worked at his features. But his resolution remained. He would escape, and destroy. One thing at a time. First, escape… He fed Kade sparingly when the gaunt detective began to stir; and not until

Kade was conscious, and the anodyne of the drugs had begun to work in him, did Wentworth himself partake of the filthy platter of food.

Kade said, humbly, "Spider, I am not worth your efforts. I must have been mad!"

Wentworth's grin was quick and ready. "Cut out the 'must,'" he said. "You and I were both mad. We must be careful, Kade."

It was at that moment he heard the tread of the guards and, jumping to the grating, saw that Nita once more was being taken to the quarters of Amoy! There was a smile of courage on her pale lips, and her violet eyes glanced toward him briefly. They could say no word, but in that glance there was a pledge. And Wentworth bowed his forehead against the cold steel and rolled it there, harshly, to chill the heat in his brain. God, let him escape! Let him get his hands on the fat throat of the man, Amoy! Down the corridor, the blonde girl was screaming.

"Blind! I tell you I'm going *blind!*"

The long hours of the night crawled past. The yellow lights flickered and went out and through the darkness, Wentworth waited in agony upon the hard board of his bed... for Nita did not return to her cell! She did not return, and he must wait all the next day before he could strike! There was no hope of success in the morning, when the guards were on the alert. No hope at all, and he must school himself to patience. Patience... *God!* Wentworth set his teeth in his arm to muffle the rock-hard sob that squeezed out through his throat. He tasted blood.

THE DIM yellow dawn of the electric lights found Wentworth's eyes burning wide-open, as they had been throughout the night. There was a hard, sure slowness in his movements and, carefully, he doled out the drugged food to Kade and himself.

"Tonight," he formed the word with soundless lips. "Tonight, when work is finished!"

Kade's eyes narrowed and he knotted bony fists at his side, sucked in a breath that arched his chest… and coughed. Wentworth appraised him narrowly for an estimate of his own strength. His flogged back was only half-healed. He was enfeebled by lack of food. Fortunate that the guards carried guns which might be scized!

The door swung open and they shuffled out to take their place on the prisoner-chain, felt the familiar cold bite of steel about their ankles. Wentworth's eyes stabbed down the corridor, but Nita's place in the file was taken by another. The blonde girl ahead of him stumbled hopelessly and kept her hands to her eyes. Tonight… Wentworth's eyes swung to the guards who marched beside him, and he barely strangled back a cry of despair. They no longer carried guns! Instead, there were only the heavy-butted whips with their leaden-tipped thongs! Could they suspect his plan? But no, it was the abortive effort of the girl ahead of him, yesterday morning. She had grabbed a gun and fat Amoy had recognized a danger he had previously overlooked. He had taken away the guns. Wentworth's jaw set solidly. Without weapons, he still would find a way! He dragged his chains heavily along beside the whirling main shaft, circled the whining flywheels. He threw himself furiously to work upon Kade's anklet-lock, and when it was prepared, he turned his attention to the machine before him. If he could detach from it some clubs of steel... but it was impossible without tools. He tested the rivets that held their chains. Impregnable. Nothing for it then but to wait—and hope. Wentworth's bearded lips twisted. The breaks in recent days had not been conspicuously in his favor!

The day dragged on and a madness ate at Wentworth's soul. Still there was no sign of Nita, and his mind leaped to wild conjectures which he held down with an effort that was physical in its intensity. At long last, there came the clank and drag of the chain and the file of exhausted prisoners began to pass by the entrance to the alcove. Wentworth's eyes flew to Kade's; warned him to relax his tension. He had to set his own hands hard against the edge of the steel table of the machine to still their trembling. His work on the locks had been sure. A jerk would release his leg. His hands... He dropped his eyes to the links of tool-steel chain that bound them together, and a thin smile twisted his mouth.

A guard swaggered into their alcove, and another stood negligently at Kade's side of the machine. The second man was watching the prisoners on the chain. Wentworth jerked his head in signal toward this second man, lifted his wrist chains slightly, and a slow hard smile built itself on Kade's lips, for he understood what the plan was, and he saw that the Spider had found his weapon!

Wentworth and Kade stood with bowed shoulders, like the other patiently-waiting, labor-drained slaves. And the first guard bent to snap about Wentworth's ankle the fetter that would bind him to the prisoner-chain. He bent... and Wentworth lifted his hands high above his head! A feeling of enormous power grew in his arched chest, his shoulders swelled… and the chains swished in a glittering downward arc! With vicious force, they bit into the base of the guard's skull, and there was no need to strike again!

Wentworth grabbed for the keys which had tinkled from the man's grasp and, at the same time, Kade jerked free of his anklet and leaped to the attack! His wrist chains swung with whining speed, and the second guard caught their glitter, whirled toward Kade with a muffled shout forming on his lips. His whip arm jerked back… and the chains struck. Their hard steel, swung with the ferocity of long-bottled hatred, caught the man across the mouth with a crunching sound. He went backward against the wall of the alcove and Kade's chains whirled high and struck twice more.

Wentworth's hands were moving with a restrained, fierce speed. The keys snicked into his wrist cuffs and freed them; a spring took him to Kade's side, and he freed the detective's hands, left the keys in his grasp.

"Free the other prisoners as fast as you can," Wentworth whispered between compressed lips. "I'll tackle the guards! Arm the stoutest men with the clubs and whips of these two guards and send them to help me!"

Without lingering to speak further, Wentworth bounded toward the mouth of the alcove! The released chain that had secured his wrists swung like a glittering deadly whip from his fist. The chain was two feet long, for the guards had had to allow him that much freedom to operate the machine. At each end was a thick bracelet of steel. The fierce armored warriors of the Middle Ages had carried such a weapon, studded with steel spikes. They called it the "Morning Star"… and there were those who spelled it differently: "The Star of Mourning."

AT THE mouth of the alcove, Wentworth paused for a brief instant while his eye ranged over the workshop. The great central shaft, with its weighty flywheels, still whined with speed. The line of prisoners extended halfway down the shop, and there were only two guards in sight. The others had vanished into the alcoves to secure the prisoners. Two guards… but they were thirty feet apart!

Kade spoke beside his shoulder. "I'll take the one on the right!"

Wentworth nodded… and leaped. Two, three bounds he took before the guard wrenched about to face him. The man shouted strongly, and the whip whined back and lashed toward Wentworth's face! The Spider took the blow across his upflung left arm as he leaped in, and the chain swung. The steel cuff at its end struck the guard's warding arm… and the arm whipped wildly, fell limply to his side. The guard staggered, a shout of pain torn from his lips. Blindly, he turned to flee—the chain swung again.

Wentworth flung a glance toward Kade as he leaped toward the next alcove. Kade's guard was down, and Kade was stooping to free prisoners from the chain. The haggard eyes of bearded men swung incredulously toward Wentworth; faces without life or intelligence gaped at him.

To this, drugs and slavery had reduced free men! Wentworth swore, and his rage went with him into the alcove where two more guards were leaping to meet him!

Bludgeons were in the fists of the two men, and the fearsome lead-fanged whips, but the Spider marched to battle at last. They could not stop him. Death itself could not stop him in time! A whip gashed into Wentworth's side, and the force of the blow hurled him against the machine. He gripped the steel and pulled himself forward another stride. He was almost within reach! Another whip tangled about his leg, jerked it out from beneath him so that he went down on his knee. Crouched that way, Wentworth swung his flail for the first time. The nearest guard screamed. His leg doubled curiously beneath him and he pitched on his face, clawing at the unfeeling stone floor.

Across his body, the second guard leaped—his bludgeon lifted for murder. Wentworth saw him coming, and his lips parted in a straight gash across. Incredibly, it was the laughter of the Spider that poured forth. Its flat, mocking thinness cut through the welter of shouts and screams that crowded this underground Hell. It reached to the heart of the guard who was leaping to the kill, and the man faltered. Fear widened his eyes, stretched his lips in a grimace. The bludgeon slashed down, but Wentworth weaved from beneath the blow and was on his feet.

The guard screamed and leaped backward. His shoulders struck the stone end of the alcove, and the Spider was between him and freedom—a thin and tortured Spider, whose back and arm was streaked with his own blood, whose eyes burned in a gaunt and bearded face. But the battle laughter was on his lips and the courage of the Master of Men blazed like cold flame in his eyes!

In desperation, the guard lunged to the attack. He flung his loaded club at Wentworth's head, lashed out with the whip. The club missed. The whip found its mark… and took no effect. Then, once more, the glittering flail of death swung. The guard screamed as he saw death sweep toward him. He tried to leap backward, and the unfeeling stone held him in his tracks. He wrenched his head aside and so almost escaped the cutting arc of the chain… *almost.* There was no need for the Spider to strike again.

Behind Wentworth, there was a bedlam of screaming and shouts; of chattering rage that rivaled the uproar of a madhouse. There were other men freed, with whips in their fists, and they ranged like avenging horrors through the shop. Wentworth sprang to the entrance of the alcove and saw a guard turn to flee… and run into a flywheel. It snatched him from the floor, an imponderable trifle, and smashed him against the ceiling.

Kade had almost finished his task of freeing the prisoners. As Wentworth watched, Kade loosed the last of them and raced to Wentworth's side. The chains swung from their fists, and red drops slid down their chilled brilliance slowly, formed small dark pools on the concrete floor.

Kade pointed with a trembling hand. "The door of Amoy's quarters is there," he said. His voice shook, too. There was a quivering of exhaustion over his entire body. "I didn't realize," he said thickly, "that this imprisonment had taken so much out of me."

Wentworth said grimly, "Come on!"

There was no point in mad haste. The screams probably had given the alarm in spite of the soundproofing of Amoy's quarters. Wentworth walked steadily, his eyes focused on that door and redness clustered in his brain. Through that door, twenty-four hours before, Nita had gone, and she had not returned. The silent tread of his feet beat drums of madness in his skull. The chain tapped against his knee, and the warm blood soaked through his trouser leg.

At his shoulder, Kade marched as steadily. Maddened prisoners reeled from their path, and even ceased their crazy flogging of the dead guards. There was that much force in the way these two men marched, shoulder to shoulder, with their slaughterous stars of mourning.

The door to Amoy's office swayed open at a touch, and they were in the corridor with the impregnable glass wall. Beyond it, the silken curtains hung straight down, and through them scarcely a ray of light could penetrate. No light, but sound came through freely. A woman was screaming terribly, under torment! Wentworth's maddened eyes quested over the glass wall and could find no break in it anywhere. He flung himself against it, and the unshaken glass bounced him backward, bruised and helpless.

The woman screamed again.

Wentworth's voice squeezed out between his teeth in a moan... one word, *"Nita!"*

Even as he hurled himself again, senselessly, against the glass, the silken curtains lifted, and he could see her sweet body strung up terribly by upstrained arms; see the cruel whip in Amoy's fat hand. And Amoy's small red mouth was smiling. He stepped back and twisted a wheel-valve upon the wall. A hissing filled the narrow corridor in which Wentworth crouched and fought,

71

madly, against the unyielding wall of glass. A hissing, and then—an awful burning!

Live steam swirled into the narrow corridor!

## CHAPTER 5
## TERROR OF THE BLIND

UNDER THE assault of the live steam, Kade screamed in agony, and Wentworth flung an arm about the man's gaunt body and dragged him out through the steel door through which they had entered. The taunting laughter of Amoy followed them, found its echo in Wentworth's curses. Outside the door, he dropped Kade and sprinted across the fury of the rebellion. No single guard was left alive, and the triumphant rage of the prisoners was spending itself upon the beaten bodies.

They yelled.

Wentworth paid no heed to them, but darted straight to the machine on which the blonde girl had labored, peered over its cupped ring. As he had guessed, the interior was filled with large granules of smokeless powder. He laughed sharply, snatched up a torn rag of clothing and made it into a bag, began to fill it swiftly with the powder. The shouts converged upon him, and he became aware of the paeans of the freed prisoners. Hands patted him affectionately; a woman fell on her knees to kiss his foot. They cheered.

"Get bags of powder!" Wentworth shouted at them. "Fill the corridor where the fat man is! Hurry!" His voice lashed at them.

He ran across the workshop with his bag of powder and

tossed it through the open doorway, against the glass. Kade was reeling to his feet. His face was beet-red, and the sear of the burn spent itself upon his shoulders. Apparently, he had caught the blast from a steam jet. His face was convulsed, but with rage rather than pain. He shook his knotted fists. Wentworth darted back for another bag, but now other prisoners were bearing their loads as he had ordered and the bags of powder piled into the corridor rapidly. Wentworth turned.

A fog of condensing steam swirled in the open doorway. Wentworth shouted his challenge fiercely to Amoy, behind his shield of glass.

"Just stay, Amoy!" he cried. "Stay there and await our coming! We will blow down this barrier with your own gunpowder!"

He heard Amoy's shout of alarm. "Fool, it will blind you! It will blind all of you!"

Wentworth threw mocking laughter at him, though his lips were drawn thin. "Bluff, all bluff!" he taunted. *"We will blow down the glass!"*

From somewhere, a packet of matches was thrust into Wentworth's hand, and he struck flame to it. Beyond the glass barrier, Amoy screamed at sight of that yellow spot of fire. He fled through a silk-draped doorway. Instantly, Wentworth snuffed out the match.

"He spoke the truth," he told Kade beside him. "The stuff would blind us all. Get sledgehammers!"

It was labor to batter a way through the tough laminated glass, but finally it gave under the repeated savage blows. Wentworth staggered through to free Nita where she swung with

*NITA VAN SLOAN* •

her toes barely touching the floor. Her back was not marked by the bite of whips, but there were red and blue bruises upon it, and small white blisters. Whatever torture she had undergone had been intended not to mark her permanently! Wentworth eased her to the floor, chafed her tormented wrists. There was bitterness in his soul. If they moved quickly, they would be free of this torture hole. But Amoy already had made good his escape while the glass wall delayed pursuit. He would have to fly far now to escape the Spider!

Nita showed no signs of returning consciousness, and presently Wentworth lifted her in his arms, draped her body in some of the torn silks from the wall. Everywhere, the freed slaves were looting the lavish office. Wentworth moved steadily toward the door. The effort of lifting Nita was almost too much for his enfeebled strength, but he struggled on. Kade was at his side in an instant.

"I found a phone," he gasped. "Called the police. Left the line connected, so they could trace it. You and I will have to be gone by then, Spider. I'm in the same boat you are until I clear myself. Here, I'll help. Damn these scalds!"

They staggered along a narrow corridor, found an elevator shaft, but the cage would not come down. They hunted farther, and there was a tight, winding spiral stairway. It was a heavy labor climbing those narrow steel steps. Halfway up, Nita began to moan. Her eyes opened, but there was no intelligence in them, only a vast shining fear.

"No," she whispered. "Oh, *no*...."

With a fierce tenderness, Wentworth whispered to her that she was safe, but the words did not seem to reach her. He climbed on, and at last came to a metal trapdoor set solidly across the steps. It took his utmost strength to lift it, and they found themselves in the vast, dark reaches of a deserted warehouse! After their long immersion in the superheated humidity

of their prison, the warm free air struck coldly through Wentworth's naked body.

His head reeled with breathing fresh air.

The shriek of sirens beat in upon his dazed brain.

"A warehouse," Wentworth muttered. "We must be near the river. Couldn't run through the streets like this."

"The river..." Kade whispered.

THEY STUMBLED off across the warehouse floor, and its roughness turned from concrete to wood. Wentworth caught the faint hollow echo of their passage, and guessed that they were over water. His eyes were strained wide and, accustomed to long hours of darkness, he could make out the vague loom of the wall ahead. But it was Kade who found the trapdoor and they peered down into pitch blackness in which they could hear the wash of water not far below. Nita stirred and muttered some choked phrase.

"I'll go first," Kade said harshly.

Before Wentworth could protest, he had dropped off into the blackness. The splash of water came almost instantly, and his voice lifted hollowly.

"It's all right. Under a pier. I can see lights between the piles."

Wentworth gasped his thanksgiving and, clasping Nita tightly, dropped into the water. Its cold ran electric shocks through his body, set him to trembling violently. They sloshed heavily off between the piles and, after a while, they were swimming....

Between the time when he was swimming with Nita, and the time when he found himself in a shack built of scraps upon the banks of the river, was a blank in Wentworth's mind. He struggled up from the floor to find Nita still unconscious, and Kade half out of his head with delirium. There followed weary hours before he could trust the drug-crazed Kade to remain with Nita. Other hours when, racked by the hunger for narcotics, Wentworth fought against the craving and staggered off to find food and clothing for them.

Fortunately, he had left some funds in the garage sanctuary, and it had not been disturbed by his enemies.

Still Nita did not regain full consciousness, and Wentworth realized that he must take her home for medical care. Desperately anxious for her, he was forced to wait until night fell again before he dared to carry her to a taxi. He made a jest of it then—great God, a jest of Nita's coma!—and it closed his throat with pain.

"These gals just can't take it any more," he maundered in drunken tones to the taxi driver. "Take prohibition times now, and they would put it away with the best of us. Just been drinking four or five hours, and she passes out cold on me. Right out cold!" And he flung the Fifth Avenue address at the driver, caught the man's quick, suspicious stare. "Service entrance," he added.

Wentworth knew well what risk he ran in taking Nita to her home, for the police kept a ceaseless watch there for Richard Wentworth. But he could not take her to a hospital without identifying her, making sure that she would receive proper care. She would be better off at home, with Ram Singh and Jackson and Jenkyns to watch jealously over her.

At the service entrance, Wentworth eased Nita to the pavement on her feet, paid off the driver, and staggered toward the door.

"You're going to lose that dame her job," the driver yelled.

Wentworth made no answer, but he was grateful for that call. His eyes, shuttling about the street, had spotted two men in a parked coupé who watched him suspiciously. He fumbled the service door open, hurried to the automatic elevator and shot it upward to Nita's floor. He carried Nita in his arms as tenderly as a child, and his eyes rested achingly on her face. It was flushed, and she mumbled meaningless sounds. Her head, with its sweetly curled hair, tossed against his arm.

Ah, God, if some awful thing had happened to her, because of him! His place was with her, nursing her back to health… A bitter smile crossed his lips. As if the police would allow him so much liberty, even if the Spider could turn aside from his quest! THE DOOR of the automatic elevator wheeled open, and Wentworth strode across the narrow corridor, punched the bell of Nita's apartment and held it in until he heard the hurried, stumbling feet of old Jenkyns within.

Wentworth held himself as erectly as possible, against the pulling pain of the whip lesions across his back; his pain- and drug-thinned cheeks were shaven clean again… but it had not seemed necessary to disguise himself a great deal. His hair was straggling, and the clothing was poor and shabby. Not likely that even Jenkyns' familiar eyes would detect the fraud—for Wentworth had no intention of revealing himself. It meant too much danger to his loyal friends who served him, Jenkyns, Ram Singh and Jackson!

Jenkyns opened the door, his old head lifted haughtily, but a strangled cry jerked to his lips at the sight of Nita. He held out wrinkled hands that trembled.

"Oh, hurry!" he gasped. "Oh, in heaven's name, what has happened to Miss Nita? This way... Oh, hurry!"

Wentworth followed Jenkyns and laid Nita down tenderly on her bed, saw how she turned gratefully, even in her delirium, to the coolness of silken sheets.

"Get Doctor Higgins right away," Wentworth made his voice rasping. "I bring orders from Wentworth!"

Jenkyns hesitated, then trotted off, and Wentworth bent over Nita. "It's all right now, dearest," he whispered to her. "All right now. You're home. Those men cannot harm you again..." He stiffened at a thought. Were Jackson and Ram Singh here? Even as the thought crossed his mind, he heard the firm soldierly tread of Jackson in the hallway—and turned to face the hostile inspection of Jackson's eyes.

"Just who are you?" Jackson snapped.

Wentworth made his hands tremble as he fumbled in a pocket. "Geez, I ain't nobody," he whined in the harsh voice he had adopted. "A man meets me on the street, see, and gives me a job to do. If he hadn't paid me plenty I wouldn't'a touched it with a ten foot pole. He give me a note."

Wentworth held out the message he had written, and Jackson kept a penetrating blue gaze upon his face as he reached for it. When he read it, he swore softly.

"Where did you leave this man?" he demanded.

Wentworth shrugged. "He told me not to say," he said. "And he didn't look like a man you'd want to play tricks on. He said bring this girl home, and I done it."

Jenkyns came hurrying back. "Doctor Higgins will be right over. You two get out of here now. I've got to make Miss Nita comfortable." He bent over her, and his old hand trembled as it brushed the hair back from her flushed face. "Poor child," he whispered. "Poor child."

Wentworth turned sharply away from the scene, walked blindly toward the door. What could any man do to repay such precious loyalty; what had he ever done to deserve it? He blundered into the side of the door, felt Jackson's hand close on his arm steadyingly.

"Better have a drink," Jackson said quietly. "You look all in… *Major!*"

Wentworth could not control the start of his nerves. It was a title that Jackson had carried over from the days when they had served in the army together on a great battlefield. Recognition… but it might be no more than surmise. Wentworth mumbled and twisted his shaking hands together.

"Reckon I do need a drink, sir," he said. "You're kind."

Jackson walked along silently by his side, ushered him into the butler's pantry and poured him a glass of brandy… and his blue eyes bored into Wentworth's face. There was anger in Jackson's blue eyes, and a bitterness in the long line of his mouth.

"No need to pretend with me, sir," he said quietly. "But, what in God's name, have they done to you and Miss Nita, sir? Listen, sir, you're not in any condition to go on the street, much less to fight! The police are always on the watch here."

Wentworth straightened against the twinges in his back. "Might have known I couldn't fool you, Jackson," he said quietly. "I'm all right. Miss Nita was tortured and is, I think, suffering from shock. Take good care of her. My orders are in that message. You and Ram Singh will take her away as quickly as possible. Doctor Higgins will go with you out of the city—out of the state!"

Jackson shook his head. "Only way Miss Nita could be got away would be unconscious. She wouldn't go," he said decidedly. "And you, sir… I never would have known you except I was sure you wouldn't trust anyone else to bring Miss Nita. You're in bad shape!"

Wentworth moved toward the door, and his smile was thin and hard. "I think the fiends who did this to Miss Nita will find I still have some potency!" His hand was on the knob when the doorbell shrilled and there was a heavy knock!

"*The police!*" Jackson whispered.

Wentworth's eyes tightened as he nodded. He had expected this! It was very unlikely that the men on watch would pass up Nita's strange entrance, even if they had not identified her!

"Open the door," he whispered to Jackson.

"But, sir… if it's the police!"

Wentworth smiled. "Just follow my lead, Jackson."

There was a renewed, peremptory knocking at the door. Jackson moved forward alertly, paused to whisper. "One thing, sir, and I don't know whether it's important. When Ram Singh and

I were on scout duty in the underworld, we saw Frank Rocker snatched. And I identified the man who did it. Labor racketeer, Lunsford!"

Wentworth nodded and, as Jackson began to throw the bolts on the door, he asked a sharp question. "Do you know how Miss Nita was captured by those men?"

"Only that she had a dinner engagement with John Lauder, sir," Jackson replied. Wentworth gestured for him to open the door and thrust the facts he had acquired to the back of his mind for future reference. *Lauder...* He began talking.

"I'm sure, sir," he said to Jackson, "that you'll find the radio works all right now. It wasn't anything very serious. Just a couple of loose connections."

The door was open and Wentworth was moving toward it. He had a pair of pliers and a screwdriver in his hand, snatched from a drawer in the kitchen where they were always kept. "If there's any further trouble, just call me, and I'll fix it without further cost to you. Oh, call it a dollar."

Jackson dug into his pocket and held out a dollar bill. "You always say that," he said stiffly. "A dollar, just to fix up a couple of wires! Could do it myself in two shakes."

"A man has to live," Wentworth whined.

The door was open, and he moved with a curious glance toward the two men who were standing there. "Pardon me, gentlemen!"

"Just a minute, buddy," one of the two plainclothesmen said, and caught Wentworth by the arm. "Where's the dame this guy brought in here?"

Jackson stiffened as under the lash of a whip. He stepped into the hall and closed the door softly again. "I don't know what you are talking about," he said curtly, "but if you wake up the mistress with your bawling, I'll knock your damned heads off!"

"Oh, a tough guy, huh?"

Jackson's head pulled down a little, and there was a merry light in his blue eyes. "Why, as to that, you're trespassing on private property, where you have no authority. But if it's a fight you want…" Jackson pushed the cop on the chest, shoving him off-balance so that his hand let go of Wentworth's arm. "You're just an ordinary guy like me, in here—and I don't like cops."

The officers weren't cowards, but they were without searching authority, and apparently under orders to make no unnecessary disturbance. They glared at Jackson and fired more questions; seemed suddenly to realize that Wentworth was no longer in the hallway and whirled to search for him; strode back belligerently to where Jackson stood ready before the door.

"Got you now, tough guy," the leader growled. "Helping a prisoner to escape!"

Jackson laughed in his face. "Don't try to saddle your carelessness on me! I'll help you catch him if you'll send him up for life! That guy is a robber, soaking us a dollar for fastening a couple of wires… Are you sure you don't want to fight? Well, so long, mugs!"

Jackson set his fists on his hips to watch the police hurry away. He swaggered a little as he turned back into the apartment… then his fire evaporated. "Lord, Miss Nita will give me Hell when she finds I let the Major get away again!" There was admiration, and a touch of apprehension, too, in his eyes. He went through the door very softly. "Wait until I tell Ram Singh how I bluffed those two cops!"

WENTWORTH ALREADY was hurrying through the city streets, and he moved with the shoulders hunched, shuffling his feet. It matched better with the poor clothing he wore; cops might question a man like him, but they would be unlikely to suspect him of anything serious. It was his assumed servile manner which had, subconsciously, thrown the two police in the hall off guard, and Jackson had played his part well. Wentworth's mind raced back to the information Jackson had thrown at him in the last minute, and he considered it with narrowed eyes.

Frank Rocker had been one of the slaves of Amoy... but he had been kidnapped by a labor racketeer, Lunsford! Wentworth didn't quite get the connection there, but if he could locate Amoy through Lunsford... He caught up a newspaper from a stand before he ducked into the entrance of the Second Avenue elevated railway to hurry back to Kade, in the hut on the riverbanks. He hunched in a corner of the slattern seats.

There were a few passengers on the train, and the guard stood inside the doors, swaying easily to the clattering lurch of the train. Wentworth smiled slightly, thinking how they would stare... or scream and run—to know that the Spider moved so quietly among them! And bitterness twisted the smile. They were blaming him now for many things. Tomorrow or the next day, when he struck at the power that was terrorizing the city, the Spider would once more be acclaimed. The public, always changing, never changed.

## THE SPIDER AND THE EYELESS LEGION

He was staring at the newspaper, with his thoughts combing over the data Jackson had given him, when a headline thrust through his preoccupation.

STRIKE CALLED LABOR RACKET
NORTH CITY EXPLOSIVES EXECUTIVE DECLARES
THAT AGITATORS FORCE MEN TO QUIT

Wentworth's eyes skimmed through the story, still without specific interest until a name snagged his attention and brought it to sharp focus… "John Lauder, New York City attorney, is handling the legal aspects of the strike for Mr. Custer, of the North City plant." Lauder again!

He hurried back to the hut on the dark riverbank and flung the paper before Kade. The detective swore as he straightened up from his pallet to scan it by the pale illumination of a candle. "Damned scalds hurt worse than the whip scars," he grumbled. "And the craving for dope! Look, I'm shaking like a leaf! God, would I like to get my hands on that louse, Amoy."

Wentworth said softly, "This may be our chance. Get this tie-up!" Swiftly, he told of Rocker being kidnapped by Lunsford, of Lauder's hand in the North City business; and Kade came slowly to his feet.

"Sounds right!" he said softly. "These petty robberies that have been pulled here don't justify the layout Amoy had there underground. There's more to it than that!"

"If he could smash the unions and bring in his own union! With slave labor he would clean up millions! Collect from both sides!" Wentworth said. "Men like this Custer, in North City,

85

probably wouldn't know his real plans until it was too late. Then they would be hopelessly involved. And the NLRB wouldn't be able to force them to rehire the men who struck."

Kade stared at him. "I don't get that," he said. "Why not?"

Wentworth's lips twisted into a harsh line. "The plant couldn't use... *blind men!*"

A cry burst from Kade. "Good God, do you mean that Amoy would deliberately blind the strikers, so that his slaves could take their places! And the owners of the plant... they'd be afraid to say anything afterward, because they might be involved! Amoy could keep the truth from them until too late. But, to blind men deliberately...."

Wentworth laughed, and the sound was rasping. "Do you think that would bother Amoy?"

Kade stared with narrowed eyes at Wentworth, then he shook his head and slumped back on the pallet. "There's nothing we can do," he said dully. "Custer wouldn't listen to us. He'd think we were playing in with the strikers or something. We can't go to the police, even if they would pay any attention to what we had to say. We have to stand by and see men, working guys like us, *blinded.*"

Wentworth laughed again, and the sound came out fiat and mocking, cold with menace. It was laughter that Kade had heard before, and shuddered at its ominous quality... the laughter of the Spider! It drew Kade up tautly, and his eyes were wide on Wentworth's face.

"Yes, yes," he whispered. "I had forgotten!" He laughed, too, in sharp excitement. "Lead me and, by God, we'll smash them!"

His voice turned humble, almost devout in its complete faith. "I'd follow you to Hell—and back again!" he said. *"You are the Spider!"*

## CHAPTER 6
## THE SPIDER STRIKES

NORTH CITY sprawled about a big loop in the Oshmatuck River just where the last rocky rapids gave way to the smooth navigable waters and dams crisscrossed the wide and shallow stream. Wrapped in the green loop of the river was the residential section, and along the flats across the Oshmatuck were the smudges of the industrial district, tall smoking chimneys, and spider-webs of railway spurs. Today there were three of those tall chimneys from which no black smoke swirled, but about the gates in the tall metal fences swirled the thick ranks of strike pickets.

There were other hundreds of men in the streets of North City and they wore an air of holiday. They were sure of victory. They had been told that by their leaders, and that it would mean more money in their pockets. Why not be happy?

There were narrow-eyed watchful strangers among them, but they paid no heed. Wentworth saw them from the small rented car which Kade drove, and they helped to confirm his fears for the thing that threatened here.

Wentworth frowned.

"Amoy is here somewhere beyond a doubt," he muttered to Kade. "We won't find him in the streets, but he or a representative will call on Custer—probably after dark. Lauder has just arrived—hasn't left his hotel."

Kade scowled over his driving. "The cops here don't know their business," he growled. "Ought to break up these corner crowds before they make trouble. These guys are armed... and really dangerous!"

Wentworth nodded his confirmation of that opinion. He could feel the electric tension in the air like the sultriness before a thunderstorm. There were police in evidence, moving in pairs, but they did little to break up the congestion. Wentworth's car was held to a crawl. If only he knew where and when Amoy would first strike! Custer's home was a logical point of contact, but all the encircling roads were heavily patrolled by the police and the grounds were thick with guards. After dark, Wentworth would penetrate those precautions, but now it was useless to try. He shifted uneasily in his seat.

"If trouble breaks don't forget to put on those goggles," Wentworth said shortly. "The rubber shields will adhere to the flesh, close out all fumes... but they will make it difficult to see."

Kade shot him a narrow, questioning glance, but Wentworth shook his head. "I don't know when or where, but... *By God, there it is!*"

A burst of shots sounded around the corner and Kade jammed down on the accelerator, his long mouth stretching into an angry slit. The coupé smashed through a red traffic light, whipped to the right... and they were in the middle of it! Men were charging from the entrance of a small bank, with satchels and guns in their fists. Against the cornerstone of the bank, a man in police blue leaned drunkenly. His hands were over his eyes, and he was screaming. One of the bank bandits paused and deliberately pointed a gun at him.

Wentworth leaned far from the window and squeezed off a single shot from his heavy automatic. The bank bandit crumpled backward across the escape path of his fellows.

"Goggles!" Kade snapped.

Wentworth swore and ducked inside to fit the prepared eye-protectors over his head. A barrage of lead slammed into the coupé. Fragments of glass flew in tiny stabbing arrows from the windshield and Kade jammed the coupé to the curb, batted open the door to leap to the street. His heavy revolver began to crash. Prone on the sidewalk, on the other side of the car, Wentworth had his twin automatics in his fists. There was a fierce eagerness in his eyes. This was the first time he had had the opportunity to meet these devils of Amoy. The Spider welcomed it!

Twice Wentworth squeezed the triggers and felt the familiar jerk and lift of his gun's recoil, sniffed the acrid odor of smoke-less powder. Each shot had scored. A second man lay struggling on the sidewalk beside the first, and a third bandit made the car with a leg limp beneath him. Wentworth drew a careful bead on the bandit sedan's gas tank... and a woman darted crazily across his line of fire! Before she was out of the way, the sedan spurted from the curb... and a siren shrieked behind him.

Wentworth called a soft warning to Kade. Despite the fact that they had struck a blow for the law, the police would submit them to endless questioning. Neither of them could afford that scrutiny! They holstered their guns as the police car shot past.

Wentworth heard a machine gun stutter into life, saw the grim profile of a policeman above the pounding weapon. The bandit car swerved widely, took a corner on screaming tires. An instant later, the police coupé whined after them. Swearing, Wentworth flung himself into the car. Kade was an instant behind him.

"After them!" Wentworth cried. "After them, fast!"

Kade wrenched the car about and took the corner behind the police. The green-and-white coupé was weaving erratically, and there were no more gunshots from it! Kade swore harshly.

"Damn it, they couldn't have gassed the men in that car!" he cried. "See, nobody on the street has been affected!"

Wentworth shook his head. He was hunched far forward on the seat with the twin automatics cradled on his knees. "You remember, Kade, the machine that mixed smokeless powder and ground it fine; and the machine that loaded cartridges."

Kade snapped, "So what?"

Wentworth smiled thinly. "I think that it is the bullets *which the police themselves fire* which disperse the gas! That machine gun loosed a lot of bullets! The cop on the street was blind… but no one else."

A hoarse shout ripped from Kade's lips as the police car swung broadside across the street, and they had a momentary glimpse of the two officers, faces buried in their hands, before the coupé leaped the curbing and ground its metal nose through a show window! The bandit sedan was out of sight, but at Wentworth's curt gesture Kade hammered on past the wreck. One of the policemen was slumped on the sidewalk, unconscious, and

Wentworth had a glimpse of the man's face. Horror ran its quivering way through his heart. The cop's eyeballs had... *exploded!*

"*God!*" Kade gasped. "To get my hands on those rats!"

Wentworth's voice came out with the coldness of a knife. "Hands would probably be safer than guns. From now on, Kade, never fire a gun without those goggles over your eyes. We can't be sure Amoy hasn't spiked *our* ammunition! He must have flooded the market!"

KADE WHIPPED the coupé around a corner, and stood on his brakes. The street was jammed with marching strikers, waving high placards in the air! Yet, moments before, the bandit car had whirled this corner! In an instant, the marchers were all about the car. They made no hostile gesture, but there were derisive grins on their faces. Wentworth peered between them and made out the bandit car, abandoned at the curb a half-block away. The men from it would have joined the marchers by now, and there would be no means of identifying them. Of the wounded man, there was no trace.

More sirens were shrieking behind them, and Wentworth let his eyes flick over his coupé. A half-dozen bullets had smashed through the windshield and pocked the hood. Kade was trying to push the car through the throng, but they insolently refused to move from its path. When the bumper nudged them, they screamed like mortally wounded men. A tire went out with a hissing bang as a knife slashed through the rubber.

"No use," Wentworth said quietly. "Abandon ship. Take off your goggles and join the march. It's our only chance now!"

Shouts of triumph arose as they abandoned the car, but no

hostile move was made against them, and presently Wentworth and Kade merged with the crowd. They passed within a score of feet of the stalled police cars thrusting slowly into the marchers. The officers' faces were white, and anger hardened their eyes. Wentworth gazed on them in pity; they were fighting forces too strong for them, against which they had no protection. And they had seen the destruction of brother officers!

Wentworth guided Kade out of the thick press of men and they hurried along a side street. "I'm going to warn the police," Wentworth said quietly. "Probably, they won't heed me, but I have to make the effort. If they take me, do what you can to keep the strikers from using their guns when the strike-breakers are brought in. Tell them what happened to the police; perhaps they will listen. Stay with them. Perhaps, after they actually start shooting, and see what happens, you can turn them back. Your goggles should protect you."

Kade nodded somberly. "What about Custer?"

"I'm going there after informing the police," Wentworth told him steadily.

Kade whirled to a halt against a brick wall where the afternoon sun struck hotly. At the end of the block, men's voices were

92

AMOY

LAUDER

lifted in a continuous hoarse shouting that had the effect of a single sullen roar.

Kade said stubbornly, "I can confront danger as well as you. I think you're trying to spare me."

Wentworth's gray-blue eyes were warm. "You are brave, Kade," he said softly, "but only one man has ever worn the garb of the Spider!—And the Spider works alone!"

Kade's gaze widened, his lips opened without words, but Wentworth was already striding away. Then Kade swore, started after him... checked himself. It was a gallant, mad thing the Spider was planning—to show himself in his identifying garb at police headquarters! There could be no other interpretation of the Spider's words. The least that Kade could do would be not to hamper him with his presence... and to work among the strikers to the best of his ability.

Kade's jaw set stubbornly and when he swung back toward the brawling of the marchers, there was a belligerent stiffness in his swaying shoulders. By God, they'd listen to him, or else!

IT WAS three quarters of an hour later that Wentworth, having visited his lodging-house rooms meantime, presented himself at police headquarters. His nose and face had the harsh lineaments of the Spider, but they were temporarily hidden under a bushy black beard. The broad-brimmed black hat of the Spider was upon his head, and in his hand he carried a glass cage which contained an alley rat, half-hidden beneath the folds of the cape he carried.

He spoke sharply to the sergeant, "I am an inventor," he said.

"I am Benito Francisco! I know what it is that has blinded these men, and I will prove it to you!"

The sergeant looked at him wearily. "Sure, sure, I know, Benito," he said. "There have been nine people in here today already to help us out. Just leave it, and I'll see that the commissioner gets it."

Wentworth shook his head and stepped close to the desk. "I will give you a demonstration upon this animal I carry," he said. "It will take perhaps two minutes."

The sergeant had already returned to the records before him. Now he lifted his head and, across the narrow width of the desk, he looked deep into the intense eyes of Richard Wentworth—of the Spider, who was known, justly, as the Master of Men!

"You will let me demonstrate this for you," Wentworth said slowly. "I think it would be wiser if you allowed me to demonstrate to the commissioner at the same time!"

The sergeant came slowly to his feet. He shook his head and dragged a hand across his eyes. "You've got funny eyes..." he muttered. "Okay... come this way."

Wentworth's lips curved in a smile hidden beneath the beard he wore. This was the easy part of the thing; the difficulty came after he made his demonstration... The sergeant was belligerent to the man on guard at the door of the commissioner's office. "Look, I know a crank when I see one, and I think this guy is the goods! Tell the commissioner!"

Two minutes later Wentworth was ushered into the office of the commissioner, and he swept a low, continental bow to the angry-eyed man behind the desk. The commissioner was in shirt sleeves, and his forehead glistened with perspiration. His scanty hair was rumpled.

"God Almighty, Fogarty," he cried. "What the hell is the idea, breaking in on me like this?"

Sergeant Fogarty said stubbornly, "This man, Benito somebody, says he can prove how those cops were blinded. He says it won't take two minutes, and I thought maybe...."

The commissioner towered to his feet. "Nine times today, already, these cranks have come...."

Wentworth said sharply, "You have already wasted two minutes, Commissioner. Why not listen... and watch?" He turned to Fogarty. "Is the ammunition in your gun fresh?"

Sergeant Fogarty frowned at him, and it pulled his bristling black hair close to his brows. "Sure. Regulations are fresh bullets every week. Me, I keep the regulations!"

Wentworth nodded. "Then pry the nose out of one, and dump the powder into this cage, with the rat."

The commissioner came around the desk. He had a paunch, but it did not quiver with his pounding stride. He seemed hard all through his compact body. "You're saying that the bullets have been tampered with?" he said shortly. "That's damned foolishness!"

"Not tampered with," Wentworth said softly, "but filled with a different type of powder; one that, when discharged, emits a gas that blinds whoever fires it! My only question is whether Fogarty has some of the ammunition."

Fogarty knocked the nose off the bullet by hammering it against the edge of the commissioner's desk with his gun butt, and dumped the powder as Wentworth had ordered. Instantly, Wentworth struck a match and dropped it on the powder. There was a flare, and the rat shrank against the far end of the small cage of glass. Wentworth stepped back then, while the commissioner and Sergeant Fogarty crowded forward. The rat was crouched against the far end of the glass cage with every hair on end. It sneezed, shook its head, began to paw at its eyes. Wentworth's smile was thin. He ripped off the false black beard, and flung the cape about his shoulders. His cigarette lighter was in his hand, and he stepped forward to the glass cage, set the base of the lighter upon its top.

He reached the door in two long strides, and turned there to stare back toward the two crouched men. There was no doubt now that the rat, throwing itself violently about the cage, was going blind in a frenzy of pain. The eyes of the two police were slow to focus on the red symbol that Wentworth had affixed, but when they did, a cry wrenched from the commissioner's lips. He whirled toward Wentworth—to look into the black muzzle of an automatic!

"Steady, Commissioner," Wentworth said quietly. "I have taken this means to warn you, because you would be apt to disregard it otherwise. I cannot tell you how to find safe ammunition for your men, but if you equip some of them with air-sealed goggles, it should protect them! Remember this warning!"

The Spider ducked out of the door and clapped it shut behind him. An alarm bell began to jangle and the shouts and running feet of men sounded throughout the police building. Wentworth crossed the outer office in a long bound. An instant later, the glass door of the commissioner's office was punched out and Sergeant Fogarty, the commissioner behind him, pounded toward the hallway with guns in hand. They plunged into the corridor, and peered into its dim reaches. Fogarty thought he saw a shadow move, lifted his revolver… and the commissioner struck it from his hand.

"Don't shoot, fool!" he cried. *"Do you want to blind us!"*

A story above, Wentworth heard and laughed softly as he finished picking the lock that sealed the elevator shaft door. He stepped inside, slid the door shut behind him and glanced with a nod of satisfaction at the steel uprights of the shaft. The building was old, and the uprights thick.

The elevator was coming up, and with a deft leap, Wentworth landed atop the counterbalance weight between the uprights. It dropped him swiftly downward, and the cage squeezed past so closely that it tugged at the folds of his cape. Instants later, he emerged into the street from the basement, and the cape was folded about his hat and coat. He was now merely a bareheaded man, with a bundle, strolling along the street.…

IT WAS just dusk when Wentworth swung his rented motorcycle from the highway and took a path through the woods toward the five-mile-distant estate of Hercules Custer, president and general manager of Master Explosives, Inc. He had just passed one police patrol, and they were tightening their lines now that darkness was falling. Wentworth let the motorcycle mutter along in low gear, legs dangling to each side to prevent himself from losing balance.

He carried no lights, gauging his way by the blue light of

dusk that still lingered beneath the trees. He crested a rise and checked for a moment, exhaust muttering faintly. His eyes sought a cluster of yellow lights far ahead among a grove of majestic trees—the home of Hercules Custer. Those other moving lights were the electric torches of the guards, and they were as thick as fireflies at sunset along the margin of a river. Wentworth's lips moved in a taut smile. Subconsciously, his hand rested upon the bundle strapped to his handlebars—the cape and cloak of the Spider. Then he sent the motorcycle coasting down the grade, toward the embattled home of Hercules Custer.

IT WAS a great stone pile of a house, this home of Hercules Custer, with wings that sprawled amid towering trees and a huddle of outbuildings like a small village. Just now, these houses were supplemented by a row of tents from which guards moved on their regular patrol of the grounds. The drawing room was vast, two stories high, and furnished in the heavy carved furniture called baronial—a lavish, ponderous room.

Just now, Hercules Custer preferred his library. He sat at ease behind an enormous desk on which papers and reports were spread. There was a vase with an exquisite pink rose, brandy at his elbow, and a tapered long cigar in his right hand. A broad-shouldered man with a massive head maned with thick iron-gray hair, he was impressive behind that broad desk—the prototype of a captain of industry.

There was an echoing hail of posted guards about the place, and Custer abruptly hopped down from his chair and trotted across toward the broad windows that gave a spreading, dusky view of the lawn beneath the trees. The contrast was ridiculous.

Seated behind the desk, with his intelligent head, his broad shoulders, he was a powerful man. On his feet, he was a juvenile, a man of quick, trotting absurdity, for his strength and massiveness was all above the waist. There was no deformity, but his height was a little over five feet, and his legs were ludicrously slight.

He stood a moment, peering out into the darkness, puffing furiously at the cigar; then, as the phone shrilled, he nodded and trotted back to hop up into his deliberately high chair.

He caught up the phone, and his voice was a rumbling bass. "Yes, yes. Lauder? All right. Send him up!"

Custer tipped back his chair and puffed smoke toward the high ceiling, and there was a small, wary smile upon his lips. He pivoted abruptly, at some sound, fancied or real, just outside the broad windows. Custer shook his head and once more faced the entrance through which John Lauder came presently, bowing in his suave courtroom manner. He showed his white teeth in a careful smile that did not disturb the waxed tips of his mustache.

"I have the honor to address Hercules Custer?" he murmured.

"You know damned well you have," Custer growled and stabbed at a chair with his cigar. "Sit. I'll have no dealings with you. Not anybody except your principal. Where's Amoy?"

"He is attending to your interests personally, Mr. Custer, and felt he could serve you better there. I have full powers to agree to terms."

"Rot," Custer snapped. "Terms not important. I like to see the men I deal with. All I know, Amoy may be a crook."

Lauder uttered well-bred laughter.

Custer scowled at him. "Get out, and bring me Amoy!"

Custer whirled his chair about so that his back was toward Lauder, turned his scowl on the open window. There didn't seem to be enough wind to stir those heavy curtains, but… Hell, there were guards enough! No need to let this Lauder see him… well, walk.

Lauder was hurrying out protestations. "Really, sir, I don't dare to return to Mr. Amoy without something a little more satisfactory! I tell you, sir, he is attending to your interests! He is planning to bring in the strike-breakers tonight, and only awaits word from me that the agreement is ratified!"

Custer smoked imperturbably, back still toward Lauder, listening with his eyes half-closed. He interrupted Lauder with a booming oath, whirled about. "Terms are this: Amoy's union will move in. He collects the pay, gives wages to the men. He guarantees satisfactory work, or I'll toss him and his union out on its ear! Got it?"

Lauder said hurriedly, "I'm sure that will be satisfactory. You need only sign the agreement for a six-month contract with his union. Here are the papers, and… *Good God!*"

Lauder's eyes were strained so widely that the whites dwarfed iris and pupil as he stared toward the window. A trembling seized his carefully-tended hands. Custer took one glance at his face, and his hand stabbed toward a row of buttons on the desk. That was when the voice spoke from beside the window, ironically gentle, but with steel beneath the velvet tones!

"I wouldn't press the button, Mr. Custer. The results might be… *unpleasant!*"

It was then that Lauder found his voice, quaveringly. "Oh, God," he whispered. *"The Spider!"*

Custer's chair spun smoothly, and he lifted the cigar to his mouth as he surveyed the hunched figure in the cape, the eyes that gazed at him directly from beneath shaggy black brows. There was no gun in the Spider's fist, but there was menace, direct and cold, in the calm posture of the man.

"The Spider?" Custer demanded grumpily. "What in the hell do you want with me?"

A fleeting smile crossed the Spider's lipless mouth. It was not a pleasant thing to see.

"My business more directly concerns Lauder," Wentworth told him quietly, in the flat, metallic tones of the Spider, "and the crook who is his master, Amoy. I hope to save you, Mr. Custer, from his machinations. Has Amoy told you how he will get his strike-breakers through the fences? Or what he plans to do to the men who oppose him?"

Lauder said, fearfully, "I know nothing of that! He... he threatened me. I didn't want his business!"

Custer lifted his brows and tapped ashes from his cigar. "Well, well," he said softly, then lifted his voice, eyes fixed beyond Wentworth. "All right, Captain. If he moves a finger, fill him full of lead."

"Aye, Mr. Custer," a sour voice spoke behind Wentworth, just outside the window. "I have him covered!"

Wentworth's smile did not waver on his lips. This moment had been inevitable since his entrance into the estate, and he was prepared for it. The cape fell from his right arm, and revealed an automatic leveled at Custer's breast!

"I have still some things to say, Mr. Custer! *Lauder, don't move!*"

Custer's eyes were narrow and hot and he leaned forward a fraction in his chair. The smoke spiraled unheeded from the cigar in his hand. "This, I believe," he said heavily, "is what is known as a stalemate. Better not shoot, Jack. I believe this beggar would have enough vitality to drill me afterward, and his gun is of a particularly messy caliber. On the other hand, Jack, do not go away, or lower your gun."

"Aye, Mr. Custer," growled the voice outside the window.

Wentworth nodded, and there was admiration in his eyes for this diminutive Hercules Custer, whose feet rested upon a special step of the elevated chair.

"What I have to say," he went on softly, "will not take long. You have read in the newspapers undoubtedly, of police going blind when they attempted to fight certain bandits?"

"When they fought *you!*" Custer amended shortly.

Wentworth nodded. "When, in fact, they fought anyone! Because their guns are loaded with cartridges which emit a gas which blinds them. Those cartridges had been foisted upon them—by Amoy! The strikers of your shop are heavily armed, Mr. Custer. Amoy's union will be a union of slaves, under the whip, under narcotics to keep them passive! I leave you to guess what will happen when Amoy's strike-breakers march in!"

Custer stiffened. "My workers!" he cried. "My boys! I only

wanted to teach them a lesson about listening to these damned agitators! You mean, my boys will be… *blinded!*"

There was a muffled thud behind Wentworth, a man's strangled gasp… and Wentworth dived headfirst toward Custer! His hands seized the legs of the wheeled, pivoted chair and sent it skidding across the width of the room. It made no sound, none that could be heard above the sudden, violent yammer of guns outside the window! Custer's chair slammed against the wall while Wentworth rolled toward him. Custer hopped out and, in a long agile leap, reached the corner against the window-wall of the room. Lauder had dived to the floor behind the desk, and Wentworth's guns were now in his fists… but he did not fire!

"One thing I did not have time to tell you, Mr. Custer," Wentworth called calmly through the racketing of the guns. "Many of your guards also are—the men of Amoy!"

CUSTER'S BASS voice answered, sharp. "Come on, start shooting, damn you! Let me see some of this gunplay the papers tell about!" His hand swept the wall, and the lights of the room pinched out. The darkness was illumined by scarlet streaks of flame from a half-dozen guns. Wentworth did not shoot. He got to his knees beside Custer.

"If you have a gun, don't use it," he snapped. "I can't be sure my own ammunition won't put out our eyes!"

Somewhere in the darkness, Lauder was squealing and Custer's deep voice boomed curses. "A hell of a mess!" he snapped. "There are swords and pikes here on the wall. I can't… I can't reach them. Oh, confound these midget legs of mine!"

Wentworth laughed sharply. This Custer was a man he could

love! He sprang erect and his hands found the crossed broad-swords, the long pikes upon the wall. He ripped them from their hangings, handed a sword to Custer, and thrust another through his cape. Then he balanced a pike across his hands, feeling the beautiful balance of the piece as he slid along the wall toward the window.

"English, I think," Wentworth's voice fell softly behind him. "No other nation ever perfected the pike!"

Custer's voice belled out. "Stop shooting, you fools, or I'll mow you down! I'm unhurt, and unthreatened!"

A gun thrust through the window and a gleam of pale light lay along its barrel as it twisted toward the sound of that voice! Wentworth's left foot slid forward, and the point of the pike struck. Its point bit into wood, crunchingly, and the gun thudded to the floor. The hand stretched and writhed and a man's screams lifted agonizingly. Wentworth's lips tautened, and he swayed his weight backward. The point tore from the wood… and unpinned the gunman's pierced arm! The screams ran off through the darkness, and Wentworth lunged through the open window at a darker shadow against the blackness. He felt the pike-point check briefly—then slide on!

There was a stir at his side, and a diminutive figure with the shoulders of a bear sprang past him to the windowsill! Custer was attacking! There was the high, whining keen of a swinging broadsword and a scream that cut off in its midst. He heard shouts of terror, and the beat of feet retreating on the soft turf. Wentworth reached out an arm to yank Custer aside. An instant later, a machine gun shredded the air where he had stood.

"Thanks!" Custer was panting. "I always wanted to swing that sword on somebody who deserved its edge! Let me skewer this Lauder, and then we'll take these men apart!"

Wentworth's voice was grim. "Lauder is gone, and there is a limit to what two good swordsmen can do against machine guns. Moreover, I doubt that Amoy is waiting for Lauder to call him. If you are going to save your men, we will have to hurry."

He led the backward-looking Custer hurriedly across the library. Custer swore. "Without that contract, what can he do?"

"He can go right in and say you gave him verbal orders," Wentworth told him, groping a way across the great baronial hall. "Once he has blinded your workers, he counts on your fear of charges of complicity to bind you to your agreement! Within a month, he would own the plant through blackmail! Damn it, he can *prove* that he did not even answer the fire of the strikers. All the damage will be done *by the strikers' own guns!* You'd have to protect him, stand behind him or face charges that you yourself were responsible for blinding your men!"

Custer's voice was fierce. "This way to my car!"

"No good unless it's bulletproof. We'll be ambushed."

Close against the outer wall of the drawing room, Custer checked to peer up into Wentworth's face. He had the broadsword in his two hands and its blade was greater than his own height. His eyes were narrowed, keen. He nodded abruptly.

"I never go wrong in my judgment of a man. Was why I wanted to see Amoy. You lead, Spider, I'll follow." He guffawed suddenly. "My God, the kids used to call me that when I was a youngster. Spindly legs and a big body—'Spider' Custer. I liked it better than Hercules. Seeing you, I like it even better! Lead on!"

Wentworth smiled and felt his heart warm toward the small firebrand. His eyes were questing over the dim room, and abruptly he laughed softly. "The fireplace!" he whispered. "It's big enough for six of us. They'll come in that window presently. They have the garage surrounded, without a doubt. Let them pass us and we'll be through their lines! In the dark, I don't doubt the swords will equal their guns. A mile beyond your wall I have a motorcycle."

CLIMBING INTO the dark immensity of the fireplace, Hercules Custer chuckled. "Another dream or two realized. Spider, I'm your friend for life! I've always wanted to ride like Hell on a motorcycle and never had the nerve to do it. My damned dignity and my midget legs! Damn it, Spider, this has to be fast. Those poor boys of mine, thinking I've double-crossed them. Come on, you crooks!" His sword rang softly against the stone.

It was fast. There was the smashing hammer of a machine gun that swept the library with lead, then the shouts of men piling through the window, the slash of long-focus flashlights. Wentworth held the pike ready in his left hand and swished out the long two-handed sword. Men poured across the long hall in a scattered line—six of them—to bunch near the far door and peer down the corridor toward the service wing. They would be sure Custer had retreated that way, toward the garage. Wentworth glanced toward Custer, caught his brisk nod… They stepped out of the fireplace, and charged!

107

The machine gunner whirled with his gun at his hip, a shout in his throat. Wentworth hurled the pike like a javelin! Its long blade cut off the shout, punched straight through the man's throat and imbedded in the wood behind him so that he jerked and writhed there, dancing like a hanged felon. The gun clanked to the floor, but there was no time to catch it up. Wentworth stood on braced legs and the long sword sang bitterly through the air. Custer fought with small sharp curses barking from his lips.

The menace of the Spider, the horror of that small man who could swing a sword so mightily, drove the killers mad with panic. There was a single shot fired, and it went wide. A moment later, Wentworth and Custer leaned, panting, on their dulled swords—and the job was finished.

"Quickly, now," Wentworth gasped.

Custer turned away with some reluctance, his eyes bright as a boy's. "Aren't you going to use that seal of yours?" he demanded. "That machine gunner now. He's worth claiming!"

He staggered a little as he walked, and braced a hand against the wall while shudders shook his small body. Wentworth crossed behind him to press the seal where Custer had indicated. Custer laughed—and gulped. "No, no, I'm not hurt," he stammered. "Only this cursed stomach of mine is weak… I never killed a man before."

There was no one at the window, and they faded into the dark shadows of the trees under Wentworth's guidance. The Spider's cape was a moving blotch of shadow, and it screened the still-shuddering Custer while men shouted and ran about the house itself. Three times they stumbled across dead men, and Custer's anger mounted within him. "My own men!" he rasped. "Served me for years. Now, that business doesn't make me sick any longer. I wish there were more of them before my sword!"

But they had left the swords behind and, instead, Wentworth carried three guns snatched from the bodies of the killers. They, at least, would not carry bullets that would blind the user! They stumbled on, swiftly, through the darkness and Wentworth heard Custer's voice break in a thin curse.

"My dog, Pink," he said hoarsely. "They even killed Pink! See, he was guarding my rose—the special rose that I bred myself and that I named for him. He was so proud of those roses...."

Wentworth dropped a hand on the small man's shoulder and urged him away from the sprawled body of the big dog beneath a rose bush whose blossoms glowed in the darkness. The march to the motorcycle seemed interminable to Wentworth, and he was feeling the drain upon his already exhausted body. Those days and nights underground had taken more toll of him than he had realized. That and the torture and the whips, and his battle against the hunger of the drugs, almost won now.

Finally the concrete road opened before the motorcycle and, Custer clinging behind, Wentworth twisted the throttle wide and sent the machine screaming through the night. His cape kited behind him, beating out small thunderclaps in the wind. The powerful arms of Hercules Custer clasped about him and the pressure of their speed thrust his breath back into his nostrils. Between his knees, the motor bellowed with power and the vibrations of their going beat all through his body. Once a police car tried to overtake them; and again a gun blasted from the underbrush, but there was no checking of their hurricane rush.

The lights of North City rushed upward to meet them as they shrieked down the last long grade and a groan squeezed itself out between Wentworth's locked teeth. Great bonfires flared about the fences of Custer's plant, and against it was the black massing of the strikers. Where they were thickest, he saw the first of a motorcade of trucks rolling slowly toward the gates of the factory!

Too late! They were too late to save those men unless Kade had done more than seemed humanly possible! Even as the hope sprang into Wentworth's breast, he read his failure in the red twinkle of guns, blasting from the ranks of the strikers, aimed at those crawling trucks. None knew better than the Spider that the bullets would strike only slave flesh, if any at all. They would strike more terribly at the men who held the guns! Already, the fearsome gas was loosed—the gas of Amoy, that made the eyeballs of men explode....

## CHAPTER 7
## BATTLE OF DESPAIR

WENTWORTH WRUNG the final ounce of power from the motorcycle as he sent it thunder-bolting down that last long straight stretch toward Custer's mills. He could hear the bass booming voice of the man who rode behind him, but the words did not get through to his brain. They had lost the first race, but the battle lay ahead, and from that he must wrest some advantage which would bring about the destruction of Amoy.

His eyes, squinted against the hammer of the wind, peered ahead toward the sprawling black mass that was the picket line of the strikers. Guns were still twinkling there. A police car sirened its way past the long line of trucks with headlights spilling their bloody red across the ranks. Wentworth thought that the police had learned the lesson of the futility of their guns, but without them, what could they hope to accomplish? Tear gas! Dear God, let them not try tear gas! As surely as living men breathed, the tear bombs, too, would be loaded with the gas of blindness!

Wentworth cursed as he fought the motorcycle for speed, but it was already doing its utmost. Their pace was a perilous thing, and the strain of the flapping cape made him sway now in the saddle with weariness. There... A scattering in the ranks of the strikers! Men were beginning to run. It meant that the blindness had struck. If Kade had followed orders, he was in there somewhere, goading them to flight, telling them of their peril. But the trucks of Amoy trundled on. The gates of the factory swung wide, and one, then another, of the trucks rolled through.

Wentworth swooped wide around the last of the trucks, caught a muffled shout and the instantly-fading crash of a gunshot. He cut his speed, began to brake cautiously. The strikers were only a few hundred yards away. Some of the stubborn fools were remaining to fight, to be blinded. Wentworth had a sob in his throat for the bravery of those men, the sheer stub-born determination. He twisted his head about.

"Can you handle this thing?" he demanded of Custer.

Custer boomed, "I'll never learn sooner. Just show me the brake!"

Wentworth pointed it out, gave the handles into Custer's hands as he gathered his feet beneath him to stand upon the front forks of the machine. He felt the powerful grip of the little man's hands take hold, shouted and waved toward the next truck in line. Obediently, the motorcycle swerved and Wentworth leaped… His hand snagged the handle of the cab door, and a startled white face twisted toward him.

Wentworth slammed his fist into that face with the impetus of his leap behind it. His wrist stabbed with pain and the jar ran solidly up to his shoulder. The man was driven out of sight, and Wentworth swung open the cab door, grabbed the steering wheel of the truck as it lumbered toward the ditch. Now if he….

Instantly, his half-formed plan took shape. He could at least turn back these trucks, and to that extent stop the shooting of the strikers. Among them might be some one man who could be persuaded to talk about Amoy, and his hideout. His eyes shot beyond the ditch and saw the hard, level stretch of the fields. His foot tramped down hard on the accelerator and there was a jarring lurch, a wrench that almost tore the wheel from his hands.

The truck was across the ditch and Wentworth held the accel-erator down, cut the wheels to whirl in a great circle upon the grass. Shots were racketing toward him from the other trucks, and they accelerated to close up the gap in their ranks. His face set in fierce determination, Wentworth wheeled the truck on. He spared a hand during that operation to slip his goggles over his eyes, and then he was heading back for the trundling motorcade. His circle had brought him close to the strikers, and now he was heading in the opposite direction to the line of trucks. Once more the lurch of the ditch and he was charging, head-on, for the leading truck of the line!

HE COULD see the pale blur of the driver's face, the furious wide straining of his mouth as he shouted. But no sound penetrated through the roar of the powerful motor under Wentworth's feet. A gun crashed its finger of crimson toward him, and he saw, rather than heard, the hole come in the windshield. He drove on… and the truck swerved wildly from his path to grind to a halt in the deeper ditch on the other side of the road. Wentworth shouted, and hurtled on.

The next truck charged straight toward him, and it was Wentworth who turned aside, but skillfully. His greater speed gave him maneuverability, and he managed to hook the front wheel of the other truck. It ripped off and Wentworth slammed past with a tearing rasp of metal as the wrecked lorry lurched toward him. The rear end of the Spider's charger slewed off into the ditch. The laboring wheels fought for purchase, found it, and the juggernaut rolled on.

The third truck wavered, then the driver leaped to the roadside and fled across the grass; left his machine to trundle on its way. Wentworth set his lips and stood up behind the wheel; took the ditch without diminishing speed. The wrench as the truck

"Get out!" Wentworth shouted at the slaves huddled within the flaming truck.

took the bank beyond flung him forward over the wheel. There
was a huge compression and jarring snap of the front springs—

but the destruction of a head-on crash was avoided, and Wentworth swung back to the attack.

The motorcade was completely disrupted. Some of the trucks were stopped, blocking those behind, while the drivers fled across the fields. Others had lunged into the ditches and only one man sat solidly behind his wheel to confront Wentworth. It took all his strength to hold the wobbling giant in the road. The breaking of the springs had dropped the weight down upon the steering apparatus. The right front wheel was twisted on its axle and shimmied.

His speed was slowing, despite the heavy thunder of his engine, and he could hear through it a multiple piercing chorus of screams—the poor wretches who were his cargo. He could not abandon them to the head-on crash that threatened. He caught the glint of guns in the hands of the driver he confronted, and they began to flame, hurling long lances tipped with deadly lead toward him.

Wentworth crouched low to avoid them, and the truck wrenched from control. It dived toward the right-hand ditch, and Wentworth flung the wheel hard over in the opposite direction. The truck heeled, teetered on two wheels like a leaning colossus, toward the attacking machine. Wentworth felt a shout rise in his own throat. He batted open the door on the upside… and that instant the charging truck struck. There was a tremendous, ripping concussion.

For instants longer, the truck teetered, then slammed down on all four wheels with a titanic explosion of huge tires. There were no more gunshots… and there would be no more traffic past this point. The roadside ditches, at this spot, were too deep to be crossed. Wentworth spilled wearily to the earth, caught up his captured revolvers… and heard an agonized scream burst forth. He whirled and saw flames lick up the side of the wrecked truck!

FRENZIEDLY, WENTWORTH hurled himself toward the broad doors which closed the rear of the truck. They were padlocked, and he lifted up the muzzle of a revolver, blew the lock loose. He wrenched the doors wide, and peered into the screaming darkness within, where the red mocking tongues of flames already were licking.

"Get out!" Wentworth shouted at the huddled slaves within the truck. "Get out swiftly!"

Only a mad bedlam of screams answered him—and then he saw the reason. The men were chained immovably to the walls! Frantically, Wentworth levered himself inside the truck, straining his eyes to see how the chains were fastened. His goggles were misted. He ripped them off and dimly made out the fastenings. All the slaves were linked by one long chain, and it was secured to the forward wall there, where the flames were hottest.

Wentworth's lips closed in thin determination and he hurled himself toward the place. Clawing hands of men wild with fright tore at his clothing, dragged at his legs. Wentworth's shouts went unheeded in the bedlam within. They were past understanding human speech. Once, twice, Wentworth was dragged to his knees. He was up again, down. The flames… Dear God, the touch of those flames!

He staggered past the last of those clutching hands, and

tongues of fire caressed his legs. His woolen clothing smoldered. Wentworth thrust the muzzle of the automatic close against the lock and squeezed the trigger, again… expending his precious store of safe ammunition. The lock held. In a frenzy, Wentworth emptied the gun, threw his weight upon the chains. The lock gave and Wentworth pitched to the floor, was instantly being clawed and beaten by a score of hands.

"You're free!" Wentworth shouted. "Get out! Get out!"

At any moment, the gas tank would blow up, and after that, there would be no saving these drugged and stupefied human beings. The liquid flames would drench them past all saving. Wentworth surged to his feet, and his left arm swung heavy and useless at his side. His right still grasped the end of the chain. He staggered toward the open doors, dragging the chain, and men fought madly against the pull of it. That chain had confined them so long. How, in their present state, could they see it dragging them to safety?

Wentworth put his head down and threw all his weight and strength into the effort. He could not hope to drag them all, but if he could get just one man pulling with him, just one… He tried to reach out with his left hand, and it would not obey his command. He dropped the chain, wrenched a man to his feet and thrust him violently toward the exit; seized another. The man struck at his face with clawed nails, and blood followed their course, but Wentworth got him up and moving.

Suddenly, they were all moving, and the chain caught about Wentworth's knees and flung him violently to the floor. The breath was driven from his lungs. Feet spurned into his back, ground his face against the metal. Then the stampede was past. Wentworth struggled to his knees. His arms gave way under him, and he could not get to his feet. He fell with his shoulder against the wall, pressed his face there.

For some reason he had wanted to get out of this truck, but it did not seem to matter now. He must rest, must… He pitched forward and the flames licked toward him gleefully. They goaded him and he scrambled on, writhing on his stomach, trying to get to his knees. Somehow, he reached the tailgate of the truck. He was, strangely, on his feet, and there were figures before his eyes. A man with a gun, and the gun was leveled at Wentworth's breast!

WENTWORTH HEARD the crash of a gun, but did not see the flame. It was strange. He was falling, falling… And he was on the ground, without any consciousness of reaching it. A man was bending over him, and Wentworth gathered up his strength, tried to strike out.

"Steady!" gasped the man. "Steady, Spider! It's me, Kade. Come on, we've got to get away from here! Those fool strikers! At first they wouldn't believe me. Then when they did, after half of them were blind, they tried to lynch me. The poor devils! Scores of them, blind. God… Come on, Spider! Up with you, man!"

Some part of what Kade said seeped into Wentworth's dulled brain. The danger, and his identity… He struggled to his feet, and there was a dull aching in his left arm.

"Wait," he mumbled. "Prisoner. Got to have prisoner!"

"Fool!" Kade grumbled. "Here, get your goggles down. The wind might pull the gas this way. Come on."

*"Prisoner!"* Wentworth insisted. He thrust Kade aside, stumbled toward the stalled trucks. One was wrecked in the ditch, and he could hear a man calling out hoarsely from the cab. It was all coming clear in his brain.

"The mob is after us, Spider!" Kade cried. "Come on, I tell you! Lord, you fool!"

But he was following where Wentworth led, and there was admiration more than rancor in his voice. A fool, yes, but what a magnificent fool! Half-dead from the beating of those madmen he had rescued, menaced by the mob, he still could cling to the one thought of pressing the battle home. A prisoner to tell about Amoy... No wonder the Spider remained invincible!

"Get your prisoner, Spider," Kade cried. "I'll hold them off!"

He flung himself prone in the deep grass, and his gun threw flame and lead high over the black mass that was the oncoming mob.

"Come on!" he roared. "Shoot and blind yourselves... or don't shoot and die!"

Wentworth heard him dimly, and a smile moved his stiffened lips. He was beside the overturned truck—could see a man pinned beneath the wheel.

"Get me out of this!" the man cried. "For the love of God, quick, before this thing...."

He strangled on the word, and there was a subdued muffled blast within the truck and afterward, mounting screams of agony. Through his tight-fitting goggles, Wentworth stared at the man. Even as he stared, he saw the man's mouth twist in agony, saw him dig at his eyes. Those eyes were glazing, swelling perceptibly in their sockets. With a shout, Wentworth wrenched open the door, reached in to seize the man by the legs.

"God, the fire!" the man moaned. "Put out the fire!"

There was no fire, save in his eyes. Wentworth seized the twisted steering post, and bent his back to the strain upon his one good hand.

"Get hold of the post!" he gasped. "Push, man—push, or your eyes will burst!"

The man groaned and wrenched his hands away from his eyes, to put them upon the steering post. Together, they strained at the bent, imprisoning steel, and his face stared close into Wentworth's, but stared blindly. The eyeballs protruded horribly, straining the confining lids. The veins in the whites writhed, swelling with blood, and a small one broke. Afterward, small drops like red tears made their tracery across his cheek. The post gave a little, a little more. Wentworth reached under the post and seized the man's legs, put all his weight into a final heave. The man gasped out a hoarse cry of pain, then his body slid free and Wentworth fell backward, dragging the man with him.

The man's hands were over his eyes again. "Oh, God, they burn, and they're like stones. Hard as stones!"

Wentworth dragged him up the embankment and then he became aware of the blasting of Kade's gun. "All right," he called weakly. "All right, Kade. Come on away!"

There were screams all about him—the muffled screams of imprisoned men, and more of the muffled blasts. It was only then that Wentworth realized the full horror of the thing that had happened. Amoy had put time bombs of his blinding gas in the trucks that carried the slaves. If they were interfered with in any way, so that they did not reach the factory, those bombs would explode, and afterward… Lord in heaven! Afterward, all the slaves would be blind! They could lead no one to the place from which they had come—to the place where Amoy was hiding his fat body in security!

Now there were screams from the strikers who had been rushing to the attack. Gazing backward toward them, Wentworth saw the contortions of their pain, saw their ranks scatter in terribly blind flight. Kade was running toward him swiftly, gun in his fist.

"Got your prisoner? Okay, let's steal a truck and get the hell away before another mob gets up its courage!"

HE CAUGHT an arm of Wentworth's prisoner, and they staggered along the road together, a crippled man with staring, blind eyes, and two other exhausted men with great goggles that hid half their faces. Abruptly, the truck driver Wentworth had saved began to scream. His agonized convulsions wrenched him free of their grip. He tried to run, to dance, and his hands clawed at his face so that blood flowed in their traces, and then… *and then his eyes burst!*

Afterward, the man sagged, moaning, to the earth while Wentworth and Kade stood, frozen in their tracks, while blood pushed its eager way out between the man's clutching fingers….

The Spider steeled himself. This man had been one of the hated whip-guards who hounded helpless, drugged slaves. He had expected to profit from the use of this horrible gas. What he had suffered was just. Wentworth told himself that, but he shuddered. The punishment was too ghastly. His hand was almost tender as he urged the man to his feet, and the clarity of his detached brain clicked on. It should be easy to turn this man's injury into a bitterness against Amoy. If he could learn a little, just a little, perhaps the Spider could exact full penalty for all these horrors!

Kade staggered. He said heavily," And this has just started. God, let me get my hands on this Amoy!"

The Spider's lipless smile was fierce, predatory, but he did not speak. There were no words for the fury that drove him against the man who could do such things for the money it would put in his pocket. No words... but none were needed. The Spider had set his foot upon a trail that could have only one ending... if he lived!

There was a new and more distant crackling of gunfire as they climbed in the last truck of the line, thrusting the blind driver before them. Wentworth paused stiffly on the step, his head flung toward the sound of the shots. They came from the city proper, and bitterness twisted him. Amoy would not lose this chance to loot and rob! And police were still helpless. If they were goaded into using their guns, they were blind men; and if they fought with their hands against criminal sharpshooters....

"Toward the city!" Wentworth snapped. "They're robbing there! And killing!"

Kade wordlessly set the truck in motion. It was a long job, turning it on the narrow road, but at last it was accomplished and they sped to a crossroad that would lead them to another arterial route into North City. The hiss of the wind, the slap of fat tires, engine roar, blended with the submissive moan of the slaves still chained in the rear of the truck. Beside Wentworth, the truck driver kept his face in his hands and swayed silently. The lights of North City swam toward them, and the dampness of the river was fresh in his nostrils.

Kade swore in a muffled voice. "I can't stand these goggles much longer. Think it's safe to take them off?"

The wind was whistling through the cab, but Wentworth hesitated. It was plain that the gas was very powerful, since such minute portions as a cartridge would release could wreak such ghastly damage.

"Better just bear it," Wentworth said quietly. "There has been shooting in the city. I hope we'll be in time to kill or follow them."

Kade moved a shoulder heavily. Wentworth was fingering his left arm, which was still almost useless. There was no wound; only a deep bruise over the trunk nerve that had caused a momentary paralysis. The truck surged across a narrow bridge, swept into a slight rise as it took Main Street… and Wentworth swore harshly. The looters had been here, but they were gone. Lights blazed in a central bank, and of the defense there were only a few punctured bodies in blue upon the pavement, and others who staggered blindly with trembling hands over the agony of their eyes.

"You see, Kade," Wentworth whispered. "They got tired of their goggles!"

Beside Wentworth, the captive driver cowered. He mumbled fearfully, "What are you going to do with me?"

Wentworth turned his blazing eyes upon the man. If he was able to think that far, clearly, he could talk. "That depends on you," he said coldly. "Amoy has put out your eyes. You can get back at him by telling me what you know."

The man was pressed hard against the far wall of the cab and his face lifted from his hands. His eye sockets were a horror, but there was a twisted eagerness in the line of his mouth.

"Hell, I'll talk!" he cried, then he cringed a little, whining. "But I don't know much."

Wentworth was silent, staring at the man. Kade said, "Where do we go from here?"

"Park in a dark street," Wentworth said quietly, "until I find out what we're going to do with this fool!"

Kade laughed roughly, and the driver began to spill out words. "Listen," he gasped. "There's going to be a meeting. Amoy called it. A lot of these labor big shots...."

"You mean the few crooks who manage at times to get into our labor unions," Wentworth amended softly.

"Sure, sure. That's it!" The driver was eager. "Well, they're holding this meeting, and Amoy was going to use tonight to prove how good he was! He's going to take over every union in the state, and the mugs will either come to heel or he'll put in slaveys. Tomorrow night!"

"Where?"

"God, I don't know!"

"Where?"

The driver growled. "I'm telling you the truth! Strike me dead, if I'm not. I…" His voice trailed off at the significance of his own accustomed phrase on his lips. "Don't… don't kill me!"

Wentworth sat stiffly erect and his eyes gazed blindly at the street before them. He heard the low, tortured curses of Henry Kade beside him, the moaning of the imprisoned slaves. In his mind, he seemed again to hear the screams of those poor blinded fools before the gates of Custer's mills. And this was one small factory! That picture, a thousand times multiplied, was what Amoy threatened.

The oath that gushed to Wentworth's lips was strained, bitterly harsh, and the driver uttered a strangled cry, babbled out his pleas. Wentworth scarcely heard him. He must stop this mounting horror. By tomorrow night, he must find and… destroy Amoy!

"Where is Amoy hiding?" he demanded roughly, but the whining negation of the driver only fulfilled his fears. Blind, he could not find it, could not begin to tell where it was. That was how Amoy would have planned it, damn his fat slimy soul!

Kade said, strangling. "We've got to do something! And quickly!"

Wentworth laughed, and tried not to hear the hopelessness of its tone. He turned to Kade… and the whine of racing auto tires cut into his ears. He whipped about. Two police cars skated into the street ahead, and their searchlights played squarely on the truck! He heard the hoarse shouts of the police, and leaped to the pavement, dragging Kade after him. Behind them were more of the police cars! They were trapped, pinned in this narrow alley of death… and Wentworth wore the long black cape, the accouterments of the Spider!

It was not of that he thought, as he cast desperately about for an escape—but of the impending horror tomorrow night. If he failed to escape now, the Blind Terror would march fearfully across the entire state, and where it passed, ten thousand men would scream with agony tearing at their eyeballs….

## CHAPTER 8
## COUNCIL OF TERROR

IN THE cabin of the truck, the blinded driver set up a shrill screaming. The triumphant yelling of the sirens drove him mad with fear and he hurled himself to the pavement, stumbled and fell, and afterward ran with his arms thrust out stiffly before him. He caromed off a wall, reeled almost under the wheels of a police car, and the blue-coated men leaped out to seize and handcuff him.

It gave Wentworth a moment's respite, but there was still no way of escape. A charge with the truck inevitably would mean injury to the police, and that he would not, could not, risk. Kade stood tautly beside him, but in his very stillness, there was a demand for help. It was as if he had surrendered all initiative in this crisis. This was the Spider's milieu, he seemed to say wordlessly, this escaping from the police… Yet his own life hung in the balance also.

Wentworth whispered swiftly, seizing on the only slim hope he could see. "Pretend to be blind, Kade, it will make them careless. It should be easy, since every other person in the truck actually is blind! Off with the goggles and hide them, strain your eyes as wide as they will go. You can blink, roll them, but never apparently see anything. I'll take all the tests they try myself, if I can. And one other thing. We must try to be handcuffed together! I think we can run in unison."

Kade nodded and Wentworth lifted his hands to his face, cried out fearfully. "Don't shoot!" he called. "Don't shoot! We're blind! Oh, blind…."

Through his masking fingers, he watched the police race toward him and heard their triumphant shouts as they recognized him. Kade pressed close against his side, in the pretended timidity of a blind man.

"Blind!" Wentworth cried again. "Blind! Don't shoot!"

He dropped his hands slowly then, lifted his head toward the sound of running feet. He strained his eyes wide, reached out to touch the shoulder of Kade beside him.

"Don't be afraid," he said, shakily. "They won't shoot!"

The police ringed them in now against the side of the truck. Wentworth recognized the bulldog face of Sergeant Fogarty— and they wore no goggles! Damn the fools!

"It's the Spider all right," Fogarty said, with awe in his voice. "I saw him at headquarters. God, think of us capturing the Spider… *blind!*"

Wentworth held out a hand, his left. "We surrender to you, gladly. In the name of mercy, get us to a doctor and see if something can't be done about our eyes! That damned gas… Is that

Sergeant Fogarty I hear? Remember, Fogarty, I tried to help you, to save all your men from this blindness!"

Fogarty said roughly, "Don't try any hocus-pocus. Keep your guns on him, men! This guy can almost vanish into thin air."

He was easing forward, with a pair of handcuffs open in his hands, his stare now on Wentworth's straining eyes. He leaped and snapped the cuff about Wentworth's wrist, and Wentworth smiled slowly. "I don't mind, man," he said. "Here, Hank, hold out your wrist, too!"

Kade stretched out a tentative right and the cuff snicked home on his wrist also. Fogarty blew out a breath so gusty that Wentworth felt mocking laughter stir within him. Even though they thought him blind, he could feel their dread of the Spider!

"Don't try any funny business now, Spider," Fogarty said again. "Come on, men, surround him! Take him to my car!"

Side by side Wentworth and Kade marched amid the surrounding police, and Wentworth did not forget to stumble and sway against Kade. A little later, Kade stepped down hard off the curb and fell to his knees, dragging Wentworth down with him.

Wentworth seized the chance to whisper, "I'll try to get rid of some of them. When I jerk the chain, start running—left foot first. And we'll use the chain to knock a few cops off their feet."

Wentworth got up heavily, started off at the wrong angle and Fogarty took hold of his arm. There was a certain gentleness in the touch. Not a hard man, Fogarty. A shame to take advantage of that, but there was no other way. The Spider must escape!

Wentworth checked. "There are men inside the truck, Fogarty," he said. "I don't know how many, but they're chained up in there. Slaves that the labor crook, Amoy, was taking to work in Custer's factory. They've been there for hours without water, without anything, and I think they're blind."

Fogarty swore harshly, and he had gained confidence through the awkward movements of the Spider and the steel that linked his prisoners together. "Bill, you and Jones and Mike there, go back to the truck and get those poor devils out. You, too, Hagerty. Sure, I know—but that still leaves me three men. Go ahead!"

WENTWORTH WAITED passively, eyes straining ahead into the night while the men trooped off toward the truck, and the other four closed more closely about them. Fogarty's hand was still on his arm. Another cop gripped Kade. One officer was behind them, and another ran ahead to open the door of Fogarty's coupé. Now was the time!

Wentworth stumbled over his own feet and went down to his knees! The man behind stumbled against him! Fogarty, and the man on Kade's other side, were dragged in close. It was the moment for which the Spider had gambled!

Wentworth put both hands on the street and unfolded his body in a high single-footed *la savate* kick. He softened it, but the cop behind him was caught on the jaw and went like a felled tree to the pavement. Kade caught the cue, wrenched his arm free of the cop beside him and chopped a hard, straight left hook to the man's jaw. But Fogarty had his gun in his hand. He struck down viciously at Wentworth's head, missed as Wentworth threw his right arm about Fogarty's legs, spilled him to the pavement and snatched his gun.

"Now!" he gasped to Kade.

They started off on their left feet, began to run side by side in perfect rhythm toward the sergeant's car. The policeman at the door had barely caught the sound of the conflict, was whirling toward them, clawing at his gun. He darted toward them… and Wentworth lifted his chained arm, swung wide from Kade. The handcuffs struck across the cop's forehead, spilled him uncon-scious to the pavement.

"Get in first, Kade!" Wentworth ordered. "Behind the wheel!"

Kade slid in, wrenched the gearshift home and, with the door still open, the car surged forward. The police from the truck were starting to run toward them, guns in their fists, but they did not fire. The lesson the Spider had given their commissioner had been too terrible. They did not fire, but Fogarty staggered to his feet… and threw himself squarely in the path of the coupé! He stood as rigidly as a soldier on parade, as a man facing a firing squad! His head was thrown back, his bristling black hair pulled down in a frown upon his brows.

"All right, damn you!" he shouted hoarsely. "Run me down, if you dare!"

Kade swore and jammed on brakes, and there was admiration in his oath. Wentworth felt his mouth corners jerk in a smile, but his hand was moving toward the gearshift with Kade's, and the gears clicked into reverse even as the car slowed to a halt under the pull of the brakes. Before Fogarty could loosen his muscles, taut-set for collision and death, the car was shooting backward, wheeling in toward the curb. An instant later, it darted forward in a tight curve away from the police!

"A man to tie to, that Fogarty," Kade grumbled. "I take back what I said about the cops in this town. They may not know their business, but they got guts!"

"Yes!" Wentworth said softly.

The sirens began to shriek in their wake, and they did not know the city streets. Kade did the only thing possible. He headed for the open country, and trusted to the fleetness of the car. It was likely the sergeant would have a newer, better engine even though all the cars were of the same make. His judgment was confirmed. Slowly, the chase dropped behind them and, presently, they could take to the back roads and slow the pace. Then Kade glanced at the cuff that linked him to Wentworth, whose hand had moved effortlessly with his own throughout the drive, seeming to anticipate his every need.

"These cuffs are going to be tough to shake," Kade said grumpily. "What now?"

"I can pick the lock on the cuffs when we stop," Wentworth said quietly, "and this is our plan of campaign! I know at least two men who must be included in any such Council of Terror as Amoy has called. Lunsford and that blackjacking crook, Upas. We will separate and locate those two men. They will lead us to the meeting place of Amoy and the others. Then, we will have to make our own plans!"

Kade nodded slowly. "It should work… and I know enough about those two mugs to guess where they may be hanging out. Let's get rid of these cuffs… Spider, I'm beginning to realize why we cops never could lay you low, and why you always beat us to the guilty man. You never give up… and you never quit a trail!"

A slight smile moved Wentworth's stern lips, but there was a warmness is his heart that expanded to Kade's words. God knew that in this battle he had known little but failures! But Amoy should yet find out how the Spider could fight!

"Take me back to North City and drop me," Wentworth ordered steadily, as the cuff yielded under his sure hands. "I'll take Lunsford, and you Upas. When we meet… perhaps Amoy will be dead!"

Kade grunted. "Perhaps… but one thing is sure, Spider. If he doesn't kill you first, you'll get him in the end!"

Wentworth's voice was low, emphatic. "He must not get me first, Kade. If he does, you must finish the job! If we fail, thousands of men will be blinded forever! You won't forget that, Kade. Come on. We've wasted too much time. Back on the trail of Amoy!"

FOR ALL its frowning ramparts and its stone Norman towers, the *Maison de la Guillotine* was scarcely a secretive place. Once it had stood lonely on a hill, but that had been when old Marie Tremaine, who had built it, was alive; and before the new broad concrete highway had ploughed its way close by the moated walls. Now gay parties danced to the broken rhythms of swing where old Tremaine had paced his doddering way among ancient tapestries and gleaming suits of armor. And a blatant neon sign on the walls depicted, in a gruesome brilliance of electricity, the dropping of a guillotine knife upon a hapless victim's neck.

The atmosphere of the place drew its throngs from the nearby cities, and there were many private banquet halls hidden away within the vast walls. It was to one of these that Amoy haled his Council of Terror, and he brought with him his own corps of servitors who slunk their submissive way through dark stone corridors. His *major domo* was a gaunt man with a patch over one eye and the mien of a gibbeted pirate. And in a stone closet that opened off the banquet hall, Amoy had prisoners....

At the head of the table, a great armchair had been set for Amoy. But it remained empty and toward it the glances of the dozen men, who had come to Amoy's call, often roved. For all the sumptuousness of the feast, that empty chair had its effect on them and their laughter was subdued, or defiantly loud, to be instantly and abashedly stilled. Finally, the feast was cleared away and Rin Lunsford, who sat at the table's foot, nodded his head to the one-eyed *major domo* and indicated the closet door of heavy oak. The gaunt pirate of a man rapped on it softly with his knuckles and, afterward, stood aside.

Silence fell strangely on the high vault of the room and for long moments, nothing happened. Rin Lunsford rose to his feet, and a few others followed him, and among them was the Pole, John Lauder... But many others remained defiantly in their seats. This was not a friendly meeting, and these were not men who had worked together. Nor were they submissive to Amoy, though he had made a name for himself in recent days.

They waited, and the silence prolonged itself and men moved a little restlessly. Upas, who had remained seated, shoved his thick body somewhat sheepishly erect and it was just afterward that the oaken door of the closet swung open. Within was only darkness, and then a shock of caught breath ran about the banquet table. A man was coming out of the dark closet, but he came like a cowed dog, crawling on his hands and knees, and every several slow feet, he paused to bump his forehead three times upon the floor, and rasp hoarsely:

*"Long live Amoy!"*

Rin Lunsford said smoothly, "I think you all remember Frank Rocker? He had quite a reputation as a hard guy, a killer."

Rocker concluded his progress and crouched like a dog in front of the huge dark fireplace, and another man crawled out of the darkness.

"Henry Kade, detective sergeant of homicide," Rin Lunsford murmured. "You all have had some contact with him. Not an easy man to handle, was he?"

Behind the captive Kade, two others walked like automatons, and one stared with blind, swollen eyes, yet carried his massive, maned head erectly for all his diminutive size... and he was Hercules Custer; and the second was a girl with a proud carriage and dauntless violet eyes, that yet were shadowed with dread, and it was Nita van Sloan—the Spider's mate!

Rin Lunsford murmured their introductions along the table, nodded his head toward Nita. "A little friend of the Spider," he sneered. "Wentworth's lady love! And both men fear Amoy too much to come and claim her! Gentlemen, rise! Amoy comes!"

The last of the stubborn men surged to their feet and Amoy came slowly through the doorway of the closet. He filled it from frame to frame, and there was a small, sly smile on his red lips. He carried a pink, lovely rose in his padded fingers and he waved it slowly before his nostrils as he came forward to take the massive chair that his *major domo* slid out for him. Amoy nodded then, and the men dropped heavily into their seats.

THE SILENCE held, and into it Amoy dropped his precisely enunciated words. "Gentlemen, I have arranged some small entertainment for you," he said. "Afterward, I will tell you how we shall organize the labor of the entire state... to our own profit. You have seen what I can do at North City, and if you have not, then Custer here, the recent owner, can tell you about it. Can't you, Custer?"

Custer's voice was dull. "Yes, I can tell them, Amoy."

Behind Amoy's chair stood the gaunt man with the pirate's face. His head just topped the high carved back, so that it seemed a living head poised there in space. There was sardonic mirth on his mouth, and men's eyes went as often to it as to the cherubic pink-and-white of Amoy's countenance. Rin Lunsford frowned at him and the man faded back into the shadows, close to where the prisoners were.

Upas put his thick forearms on the table, scowling. "Look, Amoy, we like fun, but we're here for business. Tell me one thing and we'll listen to you all night. Where we run into trouble is this. We know you got slaves that will cut you back whatever you say, but how'll you fix things so the old workers won't be hired back?"

Amoy smiled gently. "Can blind men go back to work?"

Upas' scowl hardened, then he swallowed and the sound of it

was audible. "Blind men… Cheez, Amoy, you got me licked. Can blind men… Blind the *whole* mess of them? *Thousands* of them?"

Amoy lifted one fat shoulder. "I hardly think so much will be necessary. We need merely administer one or two more lessons like that at North City, and the present workers, too, will become our slaves! But if it should be necessary…" Amoy shrugged again, slowly. "Now, if you will pardon me, we will get on with the entertainment. I have some very funny pictures to show you. Lunsford…."

Rin Lunsford reached to the floor and began to pass out photographs from a leather briefcase, appending his comment. "That's the Spider, slaving for Amoy. Here's another where he's being beaten. See? Here's a picture of Kade, and here's one that will make you laugh your head off. Kade is wanted for murder, see? Well, to show you how slick Amoy works, Kade didn't even commit the murder! Here are some pictures, showing how Kade was sapped and somebody else did the killing and got the loot. And the damned fool took the rap!"

There was jeering laughter around the table, following the course of the pictures, and Kade's head was lifted. There were fires in his blue eyes and a bitter twist to his mouth. None of the others paid any heed. Nita van Sloan stared straight before her, as if she, too, were blind, as if she still walked in the coma into which she had been plunged by Amoy's torture. The others had not changed their posture, but the one-eyed waiter was a little closer to where they stood. Only Amoy had eyes for other things than the pictures. His eyes flicked toward the prisoners and the *major domo* leaned over to prod Rocker.

"Down on your face, slave," he rasped.

Amoy smiled, but said nothing. His right hand went beneath the edge of the table and, presently, the door of the closet swung open by a narrow crack and stayed that way.

"The entertainment, gentlemen!" he said gently, "I wish to demonstrate to you how completely I control these slaves of mine, since that will be of interest to us, as their masters. Nita...."

Nita van Sloan started as if a whip had cracked across her back, and her wide eyes swung toward Amoy.

"Nita, on the mantel behind you is a knife. Pick it up!"

Nita's arm lifted rigidly and she set her hand upon a short, thick-bladed dagger that lay on the stone. She clutched it fiercely in her fist, so that her knuckles gleamed white against her white skin... and Amoy was still smiling.

"The slave at your feet, Nita," said Amoy. "The one called Kade. He is of no further use to me. Kill him! Cut his throat with your dagger!"

A tortured cry pushed from Nita's lips. She shook her head so that the chestnut curls tumbled about her face. She shook her head... but her knife hand reached down rigidly, and moved toward the throat of Henry Kade! Kade stared at her incredulously. He tried to leap to his feet, but the heavy drag of the chains held him back and Nita came toward him warily, lightly, with the knife poised.

Amoy still smiled, but his hand went beneath the table again, while the rose wavered beneath his nostrils. Every eye was focused in fascination upon the tableau of murder... and a whiplash voice struck across the drawn breath of the silence!

*"I'll kill the first man who moves!"*

From the corner where the one-eyed *major domo* had stood, a figure was leaping forward with a heavy black automatic knotted in each fist. A figure behind which flapped the long tails of a flowing black cape, and on whose head was a broad-brimmed felt hat that shaded the goggled eyes! In a long stride, he reached the side of Nita van Sloan and struck the dagger from her grip, and then the automatics swung toward the men frozen into their seats at the table—confronted the still-smiling Amoy. And the figure in black laughed, a flat, metallic sound of infinite menace!

It was only then that one of the men at the table found his voice. It was John Lauder, and his cry broke upward, thin and reedy with terror.

"Great God! It's... *it's the Spider!*"

The laughter sounded again, thinly. "You gentlemen will have to postpone your murderous plans, indefinitely," said the Spider. "Amoy, stand up... *and die!*"

Amoy's smile broadened on his lips, and he dropped the rose to the floor! The door of the closet fanned wide, revealing a close wedge of armed men! The deafening hammer of guns, of whining lead, filled the room!

## CHAPTER 9
## HOUR OF DARKNESS

AS HE snapped that final command at Amoy, Wentworth tucked his left automatic into his trouser-band and tossed two pairs of goggles behind him to Kade, with a whispered order.

It was while he was doing this that he glimpsed the fall of the rose and guessed its intention as a signal. But the answer came with dismaying speed, even as Wentworth's eyes flicked toward the swift opening of the door! His gun pivoted that way, while he flung himself aside, and a blast of gunfire sent its leaden death snarling toward him!

Wentworth caught a blow like a mule's kick in his side and it plucked him from his footing, hurled him sprawling on the floor. He heard Nita scream, heard the rough shout of Kade, but he had no time to look that way. He lifted his right-hand automatic with practiced speed, his eyes flashing toward Amoy. The thickness of the table shielded Amoy completely! Wentworth swore, carried the muzzle on, squeezed the butt of his automatic three times.

With the crash of the discharge, darkness fell upon the banquet hall—a darkness illumined bloodily by the stab of gun-flame! Wentworth rolled dizzily aside from where he had lain, saw the lances of flame reach toward the spot. There was a numbness that crept up his right side from his wound. The gun hung, tons-heavy, in his fist, and he snatched the left-hand weapon from his trouser-band, scrambled in beneath the table. Without pause then, he began to throw lead, burned it along the underside of the banquet board toward where Amoy had sat.

There was no answering cry, no crash of a falling body, and Wentworth bit his lips in disappointment. Those few seconds when hammering lead had tumbled him to the floor had enabled Amoy to escape! He had been a fool not to shoot Amoy the instant his guns were in his fists! But it had never been the

Spider's way to kill a man without warning, to shoot down a helpless man in cold blood. Even such a bloody murderer as Amoy....

Well, he was paying for his chivalry now! Pain laced its way fiercely up his side and, under the table, he crouched low and groped for a linen napkin to pack against his wound. His fingers came in contact with the leather briefcase from which Rin Lunsford had taken the photographs and, painfully, he tucked that beneath his clothing before he found the napkin. The gun-flashes told him that Kade had herded Custer into the hollow of the fireplace and they were relatively safe from bullets—but where, in the name of God, was Nita?

The pain in Wentworth's side made him lightheaded, and there was a fury that drove him on. Stiffly, he lifted himself from beneath the table and backed across the wide hall until his shoulders were against the wall. The gun-stabs told him that the guards of Amoy had sealed the doors. Guns were speaking, too, from behind the cover of the table, and a slow question burned its way into Wentworth's mind. Had Amoy planned this whole thing as a rubout? Did he want to destroy, rather than enlist, the labor leaders? But that wasn't possible. Once these men were destroyed, their organizations would fall apart. It would take Amoy months to build the association again, even with his slaves and powerful weapons!

Wentworth throttled the hard laughter that flowed into his throat. Whatever happened to him in this room, he was wrecking the plans of Amoy! Carefully, Wentworth lifted his automatic and dropped it in line with the guards about the door.

In a swift, considered drumroll he emptied the weapon. There were shouts and tearing screams, and Wentworth threw himself heavily aside before an answering barrage tore through the air toward where he had stood. He saw, with grim satisfaction, that none of the guns now spoke from the door!

Low against the wall, he began to insert another clip into the automatic. His right hand was nearly useless with the pain that worked through him. There was a fogginess upon the lenses of his goggles that almost obscured his vision, but he dared not remove them. He had long ago exhausted his store of safe ammunition, and the cartridges he used now were almost surely charged with the blinding gas of Amoy! It was likely that many of the other guns brought here by the labor racketeers were so charged. Those screams of suffering in the dark could have no other meaning!

His gun reloaded, Wentworth crept toward the door where his swift shots had eliminated the guard—and fear crawled with him. It was not fear for himself, but somewhere in this Hell was Nita, and he could not know where she was. Nor could he know whether there had been time for Kade to adjust the goggles to her eyes! If her eyes were uncovered in this mad torture-room... she was *blind!* Wentworth swore, and strangled the oath in his throat. The guns were quieting, and he dared not loose his bullets toward the few that remained, lest his deadly lead find Nita!

Wentworth flinched back from the touch of a prone body, but the man did not stir, and Wentworth groped on to find the knob of the outer door. Freedom was within his reach, but he had no thought of flight. Somehow, he must reach Kade's side; must find Nita. Somewhere in this darkness, Amoy must hide.

The wound in his side was destroying his strength, but fiercely the Spider drove himself on. With this bold attack, he had wrecked the plan to enslave the labor unions. Regardless of the fate of the men here, they would not again trust in Amoy's strength. Now, if he could only find and destroy Amoy. God, he had to!

WENTWORTH PUSHED out from the wall and he moved sideways, like a crab, bent over to the right by the pull of his wound. His left hand gripped the automatic steadily and his ears kept watch where his eyes could not. He was that way when a blaze of light reached out of the blackness of the room and smashed against him. He peered into it blindly, making no effort to dodge. He could not waste his strength that way. But his gun was restless as a snake's head, and as deadly. The goggles were thickly fogged.

"Throw down the gun, Spider," a man called mockingly. "Or shoot if you want to… *shoot and kill Nita!*"

Wentworth strangled his curse and peered through the fogged goggles. He dragged a sleeve across them, but the fog was inside, from his streaming eyes. Dimly, he made out the advancing group of guards. Four of them, and Amoy was not among them. But the man with the light had Nita clamped in front of him. The guards were dangerously close—and he could not see clearly through the goggles!

"Drop the gun, Spider," the guard yelled again. "We don't want to kill you… *yet!*"

Wentworth's lips thinned under the pressure of his pain and his need. He lifted his shaking right hand toward his head… and ripped off the goggles! Blindness did not matter, nothing mattered save Nita! His eyes probed keenly now through the shadows, and Wentworth laughed with the bitter mirthless laughter of the Spider. The gun jerked and leaped in his fist, and his bullet sped with deadly accuracy that the long years of peril had drilled into his nerves. It ripped past Nita's shoulder and smashed into the face of the man with the light! The powerful flash flew upward in a twisting, wild arc. The beam slashed sword-streaks of menace through the darkness, but Wentworth did not need them. The gun in his fist was swiveling, and three times it jerked in his fist, so rapidly that the blasting of his shots seemed one continuous sound. Yet each bullet had found its billet in the body of a man!

"To me, Nita," he called. "To me, Kade! Custer! Quickly, the door is unguarded!"

There was a rush of feet, and he felt the warm small hands of Nita close upon his arm, heard her sobbing voice. "Dick—oh, Dick!"

Wentworth wheeled and drew her toward the door, heard Kade's rough kindly voice admonishing Custer.

"I have the photographs, Kade," Wentworth said quietly, "The pictures that will prove your innocence!"

"To hell with that," Kade snapped. "A lot of them are dead. Lauder is dead—but Amoy got away! He was at the outer door before you hit the floor the first time! How you ever dodged those bullets…."

Wentworth laughed sharply. He could not let them know of his wound. They were in the hallway, and he could hear the rumors of the panic that shook the *Maison de la Guillotine*. Never mind that now. There was a back exit he had found, by which he had made his entrance to overpower the one-eyed *major domo* and take his place. And Amoy was escaping....

"Quickly!" he panted, and it was his pain that made his heart race, and his breath labor. "Hurry, I know where Amoy has gone!"

Kade swore and took the lead. It was time, for Wentworth was stumbling and there were flashes of fiery light that blotted out his vision, but were caused by the pain within his eyes! When he staggered out into the coolness of the night air, he could see only the brilliant neon glow of the dropping knife of the guillotine. His eyesight was being cut off like that. Grimly, Wentworth faced the certain knowledge that he was going blind. Pain was beginning to eat at his eyes, and he had to grip Kade's arm to run the last yards to the car. He groped his way inside.

"Back to North City," Wentworth gasped. "And make all possible speed, Kade. All possible speed."

He slumped back against the cushions and his left hand, which still gripped his gun, was about Nita's shoulders. He felt them quivering under his touch.

"Oh, Dick!" Nita whispered. "Oh, Dick, I don't know what happened to me! I remember only that awful hole beneath the earth, and the torture. And then I heard your voice a little while ago, and saw you fighting with them before the lights went out. It is awful not to... not to *know!*"

"Drugs," Wentworth reassured her softly. "That and shock. They must have come for you again after I took you home, over-powered Jackson... Careful, my dear, Kade knows me only as the Spider. I have been careful that he should have no chance to identify me for, presently, he will be a cop again."

NITA STRAIGHTENED, stilled her sobs—and the car moaned with speed, hissed with the whipping of the cool night wind. Nothing could cool the burning in Wentworth's eyes. Like a rising tide, the waves of agony increased. His teeth were shut on his lower lip. How long before his eyeballs burst? But that did not always happen. Perhaps, he had suffered only a light dose of the gas. Perhaps... He lifted a cautious hand to his eyes and the pupils were swollen, hard as rock!

Well, he had made what little preparation he could for this eventuality. The newspapers termed this blindness "a mechanically induced glaucoma." Wentworth knew that, if too great physical damage was not caused to the actual machinery of the eye, doctors had sometimes accomplished cures of normal glaucoma. Such damage was caused by the pressure of infused fluids within the eyeball, which disrupted the tissue. Wentworth had with him a small vial of pilocarpine which, by contracting the pupil, would somewhat relieve the pressure in the tiny canals of the eye. Carefully, lest Nita see and suspect his blindness, Wentworth instilled a few drops of the liquid into each eye.

It was difficult in the speeding car, with Nita so close beside him, but she made no comment. Afterward, Wentworth strained the lids shut over the swollen, rock-hard balls. Complete rest, too, was part of the treatment. Rest—for the Spider? Wentworth fought down the jeering laughter that rose to his lips. He set his hands on his knees and they knotted into hard fists. The ache of the bullet wound was as nothing compared to the pain of his eyes. That wound was not terribly severe, could not be, or even the iron will of the Spider could not have kept him on his feet!

"We're pretty close to the city," Kade called. "Where do we go now?"

"Custer's estate!" Wentworth called back.

"You're crazy, Spider! Custer here says he doesn't know where he was held prisoner!"

"Custer's estate," Wentworth repeated sharply. "Amoy had a pink rose in his hand, of a special kind that Custer himself has bred, and which grows only on his estate. Amoy *has* to be there! But make it fast, Kade!"

Kade swore, and there was admiration in his voice for Wentworth's keen observation and deduction, but Wentworth's lips once more were shut thinly against the pain.

"Nita," he controlled his voice by an effort. "I don't know whether your eyes were exposed to the gas in there but I have a liquid here. Put a drop or two in each eye as a precaution."

Nita whispered, "Yes, Dick!" Her cool tremulous hand met his and took the small bottle with its dropper. Wentworth leaned back against the cushions and felt presently that the pain in his eyes was easing a little—and it was time! He calculated that they were drawing close to the Custer estate, to the hideout of Amoy!

"When you see the lights of Custer's place," Wentworth called softly to Kade, "go slowly up the next grade. About halfway up, you will find a narrow lane. Stop there, and I'll go on alone! Wait, Kade!" Wentworth stilled the protest that grumbled to Kade's lips. "Here are the photographs of the murder for which you are held responsible. They will clear you—and afterward, the police will listen to what you have to say. Warn them of Amoy's bullets and what they can do. Tell them to get consignments of revolvers and ammunition from Europe. I know of no other safe supply, for Amoy has scattered his ammunition everywhere!"

Wentworth rode down Kade's muttered objections and hammered on. "I want you to take Miss van Sloan and Custer back to New York as witnesses against Amoy. Then, if I fail, you may be able to build a case against Amoy!"

Kade finally got his chance to speak. "Why not let me go along now and make sure of Amoy?" he growled. "Damn his black soul... Begging your pardon, Miss van Sloan, but you could drive the car back to New York and file information against Amoy."

Nita made no answer, but her hand crept into Wentworth's and clung there, coldly. Wentworth answered quietly.

"One man is safer than anything less than an army," he said curtly. "You're good, Kade, but you're not an army!"

Kade grumbled, but when the car slowed to a halt, he did not again demur.

Nita clung to Wentworth. "You saved my life, Spider," she said brokenly. "I want... I want to thank you!"

Wentworth did not need his vision to know that she was waiting for his kiss, and a strong trembling shook him. He knew, without question, that this time the Spider went surely to his death. For the last time on this earth, then, he would hold Nita in his arms, and he could not speak... He could not even see the dear sweetness of her face and lifted lips! His hands were heavy at his sides, but he lifted them hesitantly, and groped for her kiss in the darkness and the pain that was closing in upon him so terribly. The warmth of Nita's lips shook him like the shock of a bullet. His arms tightened—and a stab reminded him of his wound! She must not feel the wet stains upon his side. He drew back quickly.

"Goodbye, my dear," he said gently. "You are... are very sweet."

He caught the strangled sob on Nita's lips, stepped back another quick pace and almost fell into the ditch! After that, he stood rigidly, lest his movement betray his blindness.

"Good luck," Kade called. "You're all man, Spider... and I'm following orders, though I don't like it. By the time I reach New York, you'll have everything sewn up!"

Wentworth's lips twisted. Perhaps it was a smile. "Good luck, Kade!" he whispered.

He heard the motor start quietly, and the whine of tires as the car curved in the broad roadway and gathered speed over its back trail. And Wentworth did not stir, for Nita would be looking back, and he must make no awkward movement that would betray him. His eyes burned... Tears! Good God, *tears* after all this....

Nita was twisted about on the rear seat of the car, and she could not hold down the sobs that strangled her, though she thrust her hands hard against her lips. She did not try to look backward toward where Wentworth stood in the gloom of the wood's edge, and her hands lifted to brush against her lids.

"Don't you worry about him, Miss van Sloan," Kade called cheerily. "That man is indestructible. I've been in some tight holes in my life, and tighter ones with him, and he worms out of them like *nothing!* That Spider is all man!"

Nita's head lifted and there was a slight, tremulous smile on her soft mouth. "Oh, yes!" she whispered. "Oh, yes! But it was... hard to see him go that way, alone!"

She stared straight before her, but her eyes were closed, and there was a strange hard swelling behind the lids. When she lifted her hand to touch them again, they were stone-hard. But the agony in her eyes was nothing to the pain in her heart. Hard to see Dick go, alone, but she would have only been a burden to him. He would need all his wonderful brain where he was going; and he could not spare his keen eyes for her... for Nita, who was blind!

AT THE roadside Wentworth sat to remove his shoes so that he could better follow the path. Afterward, he moved stolidly toward the woods lane he had traveled twice before on the motorcycle. He blotted out all other thought, even of Nita speeding away to safety in New York City—Nita, whom he would never see again, even if he survived! Better this way. Better that Nita should never see his blind, staring eyes, and his helplessness.

He closed his mind to the thought.

Somehow, blind, he had to find his way to the Custer estate before dawn. He would know when light was nearby the brisk caroling of the birds. He would hide among the shrubbery, as near the Custer house as possible, until he heard Amoy speak, and then… Wentworth's hand clamped hard about the butt of his automatic. His aim had never failed him before—in darkness or in light! It would not fail him this time! What happened to the Spider afterward would not matter very much….

The Spider's cape did not bell from his shoulders with his speed now, for he walked with groping hands outthrust before him and felt for the twists in the path with his unshod feet. Time and again, he stumbled, and twice fell to his knees, yet pressed on… Weakness worked upon him and he knew the drain of long hours of battle, and ceaseless vigilance and pain. He was no gallant, bounding figure this time as he went into battle, but never had the Spider held his head more erect, or borne his shoulders more proudly. There was something inevitable and resistless about his ponderous march, and his will was unfaltering though he knew this trail led but to death! The Spider marched, as of old… only the keen eyes did not gleam beneath the menace of his brows. They were closed upon his suffering.

In the fiercely concentrated effort of remembering the turns of the path, and the direction of the estate, Wentworth walked, unknowing, into a glare of auto headlights focused upon the lane! There was an instant's still surprise among the armed men who lay in ambush about the spot—then the guns fell surely into line!

It was at that moment that Wentworth stumbled over some trifling obstruction in his path. His arms swung out, wildly groping… and the gun did not fire. But a man sprang suddenly from the bushes beside the path and struck viciously with his gun at Wentworth's head—and laughed as the Spider pitched forward!

A pent breath like a sigh gusted from Wentworth's lips and his cape fluttered up from his shoulders, settled gently over his gauntly weary body. Almost gratefully, he seemed to sag to earth. His hand came somehow beneath the calm face, drawn now with fatigue and pain, as if he were a child asleep. Where the gun butt had struck, a tiny red bead formed.

It slid across his temple and made a dark spot in the soft white swirling dust.

"Ho!" cried the conqueror of the Spider, laughing. "Ho, I guess we won't have some fun now with this high and mighty Spider! The dog is *blind!*"

## CHAPTER 10
## WHEN THE BLIND COMMAND

A MOY PILLORIED the captive Spider through the underworlds of half the upstate cities of New York. Draped still in the robes he had made a living terror to all crookdom, Wentworth was exhibited, a blind and helpless prisoner, to help restore to Amoy the prestige which had been stripped from him by the Spider in that brief, terrible battle at the *Maison de la Guillotine.*

Wentworth's wounds healed in that slow, humiliating pilgrimage, but to Amoy the wounds that he inflicted on the Spider's pride seemed enough to break even the Spider's fiery spirit! The Spider's blind face was an expressionless mask and he obeyed the most arrogant commands of his captors—but it was well that his eyes showed nothing! It is doubtful if even the bitter strength of the Spider's will could have concealed the fury, the steady purpose that burned more hotly day by day as he trod his own brutal *via dolorosa*. It was a travail that would have broken the spirit of any ordinary man; that would have driven a strong man mad. But the Spider deliberately humbled himself... and waited!

It was as if Amoy sensed that hidden purpose, for while he heaped indignities upon his prisoner, he never relaxed his hard watchfulness. The chains were never struck from Wentworth's wrists and feet, and three guards watched him day and night. Twice Wentworth had stripped him of his carefully built cohorts. Twice Amoy had laid considered plans which could not fail... and yet had broken on the rock of the Spider's strength! Now, Amoy was almost ready to strike again, and this time he could not fail. He would kill the Spider before the attack began!

So Amoy taunted the Spider night after night when he exposed him in secret places to the ridicule of the underworld... secret, because the efforts of the Spider had set the police upon Amoy's trail!

"You have too few lives, Spider," Amoy taunted him. "How can I make you pay separately for these many inconveniences?"

And Amoy jeered: "I shall make you crawl, Spider, and beg for mercy. Before you die, you shall be glad to cry, '*Long live Amoy!*' if it will earn you release!"

The powerful, the all-conquering, the helpless Spider

listened—and the proud stony mask of his face gave no sign of the will behind it.

"I wish, Spider," said Amoy almost fretfully, "that you had your eyes back for a while. I'd like to look into them and read your heart—before I plucked them out again!"

Wentworth answered him, "What is there to read in the heart of a slave, Amoy?" The humbleness of his accents was a taunt. "Surely, I serve you well! Look how many have flocked to your banner since I am your slave! Don't I amuse your friends?"

So Wentworth's lips formed the words, and his lids hid his blind eyes—and there was a coiled-spring watchfulness in him that never died!

Amoy's fear would not let him rest. Day by day, he increased his torments... and did not relax the guard. And the Spider, blind, bided his time as, in ancient times, blinded Samson must have labored at his slavish tasks and waited for his day in the temple....

They had been in Morgantown now this last week and, as always at night, the great and near-great of the underworld came to Amoy's quarters to see the torment of the Spider. They never tired of seeing him drag his chains across the floor, or trying to wring from him one cry for mercy, one grimace of rage of despair. But, as always, they ended by striking and beating the helpless gaunt man in chains. Inwardly, Wentworth smiled at their rage, for he knew that they did this because, even in chains, the Spider daunted them. And he knew that they were wise in their fear!

BUT ON this night there came an interruption to the torment.

A man ran into the underground room which was ever Amoy's preference, and Wentworth's sharpening ears knew from the confused swiftness of his footbeats that he ran in fear!

"Amoy!" the man cried. "Amoy, I got some news from New York. That guy, Kade…."

"Later," Amoy said offhandedly. "Kade can wait!"

But he made an opportunity soon to hear the man's report while Wentworth, watched over by his three guards, stood near almost forgotten in the moment of tension. So Wentworth's blind man's ears caught the words that were whispered harshly to Amoy!

"Amoy, listen! Kade has been back in New York a month," the newcomer said rapidly. "You know that. He got those pictures you had and the police have been checking all this time. Well, he's been cleared and reinstated!"

Wentworth could almost see Amoy's slow, fat shrug. He heard the chair creak to the movement. "You interrupt me with this foolishness?" Amoy asked ominously.

"There's more," the man hurried on. "They believe him about your bullets!"

"So? Police afraid to use their guns bother me even less than the fools who do… and are blinded!" Amoy said silkily. "The wild shots of blind men sometimes hit people!"

"But Amoy…."

Wentworth choked his laughter. He knew the rest of the message, and knew that Amoy's time was drawing near an end. The police were flying ammunition from Europe!

Wentworth hurled himself toward the leader of the guard!

"Perhaps now is the time," said Wentworth softly, "when I should cry, 'Long Live Amoy!'"

Amoy's feet thudded on the floor. His palm cracked against Wentworth's mouth. "Dog!" Amoy whispered. "You did this to me! You, and no one else! I should kill you now, but it is too soon. I shall only beat you a little, myself!"

The whip hissed through the air and bit into the crisscrossed weals of Wentworth's back, but Amoy's strength was less than that of the guards who had lashed him so many times. Wentworth stood straight beneath the blows, his face stony as always, and his thoughts raced. Soon now, he told himself—oh, soon—his hour would come!

His imperviousness to the beating infuriated Amoy, so that the fat man bent toward him. Wentworth caught the scent of his perfume, and Wentworth's hands clenched alertly on his chains… Amoy cursed and retreated hurriedly.

"I will tell you how badly you have failed, Spider!" he cried, and his voice rose thinly. "My plans are already made! Tomorrow, at the noon hour, your guards will take you to the central square of Morgantown, and hang you in all your glorious robes. I have even had fresh garments prepared for the occasion, so that you shall do me honor! While you struggle in the noose, you will hear shots and screams… and you will know that the men your humble presence has brought to follow me—are looting every bank in the city!"

Wentworth said mockingly, "Strangled, how shall I cry 'Long Live Amoy!'?" If he goaded Amoy to reveal all his plans….

"You mock me, fool!" Amoy's voice was shrill in rage. "You

will learn how great I am! How do you think I outwitted you if I have not foresight? There are such things as gas bombs which do not contain tear gas! There will be thousands of people in the square tomorrow when you hang. Thousands! Tell me, Spider, how will the police pursue us through the ranks of thousands of blind men and women, who will mill in their path? Milling and screaming through the streets while the gas eats out their eyes!"

Amoy laughed, and crashed the whip down upon Wentworth's head so that he plunged, half-conscious, to the floor.

**THROUGH THE** long night, Wentworth fought for some plan by which he could warn the people or kill Amoy—and no plan came to him in his despair. The change of guard, the stirring of men, told him finally that day had come, but no one approached his cell until at last a guard thrust rustling clothing in.

"Time to get dressed, Spider," he laughed coarsely. "You're going to dance… a dance on air! Spruce yourself up, Spider! Get dressed to kill!"

Wentworth pretended a fumbling fear as he slowly donned the garments provided for him. The shirt had been slit under the arms so that his chains need not be removed.

There was a cape to throw about his shoulders, and a broad-brimmed hat to draw down over his blind eyes. He was ready. The hour must be ready for Amoy's attack—and still the Spider had no plan! Was it, then, the intention of Amoy to hang him in these chains which blocked his every hope of escape? He dared not ask, yet its importance to him was overwhelming. Only with the chains removed would he stand any slightest chance of winning free, of warning the populace—and killing Amoy! His only recourse was to make the guards think him finally broken in spirit, to convince them that the Spider was a coward!

"It's an awful fate, to be hanged in chains," Wentworth whined at the guard.

The guard laughed, poked at him with his whip butt as if he were a caged animal. More than once, Wentworth had been tempted to seize that whip as a weapon. But even if he struck down the guard, he could not be free of chain and cell. The man on guard never had the keys. Only when all three guards were together could he be sure that the keys were at hand. And for a blind man, chained and unarmed, to overpower three armed guards when other men were within call!

The feet of men were tramping irregularly toward him now, and Wentworth carried on his pretense of terror, cringing back in the corner of his cell, fighting futilely.

"Come on now, Spider, be nice," the guard jeered. "It will be over soon. Just a nice little noose around your throat once you get up on the ladder, and a nice little dance on thin air!"

Wentworth knew by the varying tones of laughter that all three guards were present. The keys were at hand, because his cell door was unlocked. He teetered to his feet, and his ears reached beyond the men, listening. The voices of a score of others were muttering just beyond the corridor door, but he could not distinguish the silky thin exactness of Amoy's speech. Wentworth sucked in a slow breath. Not yet, not yet!

Two of the guards seized his arms and thrust him forward and another prodded his back with a gun muzzle. No relaxation in precautions, even now when they were ready to hang him! A door creaked open and the staleness of tobacco odor and whiskey drifted into his face. The increased volume of voices told him the tension of these men, and their laughter was boisterous.

"Long live the Spider!" one mocked, and laughter made the room shake.

A man sloshed the dregs of a glass of beer into Wentworth's expressionless face. A rope was noosed about his neck, so that the end trailed as he was marched on. Men yanked and stepped on that trailing noose-end until Wentworth was half-strangled. A violent kick sent him sprawling, and a heel ground into the back of his supporting hand. And Wentworth could not now allow himself the dignity of pride and calmness under these torments. Above everything else, he must make his three guards contemptuous of him. It would have taken less courage to hold his head high, to hurl himself madly upon his persecutors. The Spider had the courage to grovel on the floor!

He was yanked up off his knees, and the bedlam of voices cut off. The rope was lifted from his neck.

"He'll swing soon enough, and we don't want nobody to get suspicious on the street," the guard behind him growled. "Will Amoy be there?"

"Hell, no. Think he'd risk his fat neck?"

"Silence, fool!"

Wentworth strained his ears. The men in the room they had left were quieter, and one voice was lifted above the others, authoritatively—but it was not Amoy. They were getting ready to leave, to spread their gas of blindness among the helpless thousands of the square! Wentworth's teeth sank into his lip with the effort at control. Everything in him urged an immediate break for liberty, but cold reason told him it would be futile. Suppose he reached the street? He would not know which way to turn even to find a telephone! Before he could accomplish anything, they would strike him down. Patience! If he went submissively, they would take him to the square to hang him, and that would be the place where best he could give the warning. Surely, the thousands would heed the warning shout of the Spider with a rope around his neck!

AT THE careless command of his guards, he crouched low on the floor of a sedan and the car got underway with a smooth spurt of power. But two men still kept their hands upon his arms.

"Don't try no funny stuff, Spider! We got guns in our fists, and we'll use them!"

"Do you think I'm crazy?" Wentworth snarled. "I'm not going to get myself shot!"

The guard guffawed. "That's right, Spider! You're going to get yourself hung!"

Wentworth heard the hoarse wails of a fire siren, the mournful hoot of a tug upon water. The mutter and rumble of traffic was all about him, and he could sense a growing tension in his guards. He lifted a chained hand to his forehead... and suddenly realized that hand was trembling! Deliberately, he increased that tremor, made his whole body shake—but his soul was sick within him. In God's name, was he suddenly afraid? He, the Spider, frightened?

A guard prodded him. "Cheer up, Spider, it will be over

soon." There was even a shade of pity in his contempt. "Pete, can you imagine us ever being afraid of this punk? He ain't got the guts of a rabbit! Look at him shake!"

Wentworth bowed his head between his knees and made no answer, forced cold thoughts through his brain. What was this trembling? He could still calmly confront the idea of death, so it was not that. It was… It was the echo of traffic about him that was frightening! Suddenly, he understood his tremors. He was a blind man, and it was a blind man's terror that shook him. The fear of the unseen things that could crush and maim him. And he was prey to that—he, the Spider, for whom death itself had no terrors!

Scornfully, he brushed the thought aside, concentrated on his escape. The guards would be on the alert every minute until they got him on… it was a ladder they had mentioned, wasn't it, with a rope around his neck? Not until then would their vigilance relax for a second. His hands clenched together. He must wait, then, until they had him on the ladder, with the noose ready. It was a thought that did not bother him, for a grim smile crossed his lips. No, his hesitancy had been of another sort. It was the idea of dashing, blind, into the street that had intimidated him. Well, that too lay ahead, for the men had said that Amoy would not be present at the square, and the Spider must find Amoy!

The traffic fell away from about the car, and there was a fresher scent to the air, even a smell of water. They had entered the park! He caught a faint whisper of the guards.

"That lamp post right in the middle, Amoy said!"

Wentworth felt coldness touch his heart at those words, but

it died in his immediate anger. He mocked himself bitterly. The Spider was angry at himself that, blind and chained, about to be hanged, he could know his moment of fear! And he dare not allow himself even a show of courage, lest he win not even his moment upon the ladder! No, he must keep up his semblance of terror… and, at the same time, steel himself to cold courage! Even the Spider had never met such a test before!

The car jerked to a halt, and Wentworth heard the man in front leap to the earth, while the other two tightened their holds on his arms. Everything within Wentworth urged him to leap and strain against their hold, to launch his attack. No, no—not yet. The third man was apart. He could shoot him down… and it might be the third man who had the keys!

"Quick!" he heard the voice of the third man. "Quick, now. You, Mike, grab him and carry him up the ladder. I'll have the rope ready. Damn Amoy! He would give us a job like this!"

Wentworth squirmed, but without any great exhibition of strength.

He let all his weight sag against the strength of the guard, so that a second man seized his legs while the first struggled to mount the ladder. But Wentworth dared not make it too difficult, lest they merely toss the rope over the post arm and drag him up by the neck. That would destroy his last hope! He took it out in whimpering, in twisting his head from side to side. The hands were free of his legs. That meant he had mounted higher than a man's head. The guard who held him was struggling upward, panting.

"For God's sake, Spider," he swore irritably. "Get your feet on the rounds, or I'll throw you down!"

It suited well with Wentworth's plans. He whimpered assent. "Look, you don't have to hang me," he pleaded eagerly. "Just pretend to. Tell Amoy the rope broke or something! Look, I'll climb! You don't have to worry!"

"Sure," the man said roughly. "I'll tell Amoy the rope broke!"

"Hurry, you damned fool!" an urgent voice called upward, and Wentworth spotted the location of one man on the ground.

"The rope's tied! Hurry!" shouted the second—and this one, too, Wentworth spotted.

WENTWORTH FELT the guard let go with one hand, heard him grunt as he reached for the swinging noose above their heads. Wentworth sucked in a quick breath. This was the moment, the instant he had played for throughout the long days and nights of torture, hiding his true strength, masking his steely will under a cringing mask. He sucked in that breath… and the Spider went into action!

The quick dart of his chained hands found the body of the guard beside him on the ladder. Wentworth's legs were braced against the rungs and his body was set for the effort. All his strength went into a single deft powerful heave of his shoulders! There was a startled shout as he tore loose the man's hold on the ladder. Then Wentworth hurled him bodily through the air, a human missile, toward the voice of the leader of the guards! Even as he acted, he heard a strangled shout from the earth and knew that he had gauged his direction exactly!

For the moment, those two men would be out of the battle;

perhaps one of them might be knocked out, but there was a third armed man, and not for a single instant could the Spider delay! He did a thing which tried his blind man's courage to the utmost. Without hesitation, he pushed out from the ladder—and jumped into space! He leaped toward the invisible earth, toward the third of the guards who had cried up that the rope was ready to hang the Spider!

Wentworth's chained hands were lifted high above his head, and his feet were thrust out stiffly before him so that he went plunging like a projectile toward the earth he could not see—toward the guard whom he must overpower or die! The mingled first shouts of the three guards were still upon the air when he heard the thudding impact that cut off some of the cries, and exultation throbbed through Wentworth's heart, for that first blow, at least, had gone home!

In the next split-second, Wentworth's feet gouged into a human body, drove the third guard to earth. The Spider whipped down his chained hands with all the strength and pent-up hatred of his soul! The chain make a faint hissing in the air, and the sound stopped with a crunching thud!

Wentworth struck the earth awkwardly, with an arm twisted painfully beneath him, his legs wrenched by the shock. He pitched sideways and the breath was driven from his body, but he was already in scrambling motion. If only he could see! He knew that he had bowled over the three guards, that the one immediately beneath him was probably dead, but the momentary respite was not enough. Before they recovered… Wentworth's hands pawed frantically over the body beneath him in search of a weapon, of the key that would release his chains. A sob of anguish jerked at his throat. He couldn't find the revolver!

By a violent effort, Wentworth controlled his apprehension. Of course! The man would have had the gun in his fist! It might have been thrown anywhere! Violently, Wentworth wrenched the body over and groped for the hands. Behind him, he heard a groan and a muffled curse! At least one of the two remaining guards was still alive—and he could not find the gun!

With an oath that had its rasp of frenzy, Wentworth hurled himself toward the sound of that moan! His foot slipped, and he plunged to the earth. Breathing hard, he crept on hands and knees to the attack. If only he could *see*... A blow grazed his cheek, but it was weak and ill-directed. Wentworth laughed harshly, triumphantly! On his knees, he lifted his chained hands again and a panic-stricken scream beat up against his face as he swung the chain downward! Afterward, there was silence—and this time his groping hands found a gun, found another and a handful of ammunition in the guard's pocket.

There were cries in the distance now. Wentworth's hands trembled with the blind need for haste as he fumbled over the bodies of the guard. There was no sign of life in any of the three. It was plain that he had killed one in the fall from the ladder. He found no more guns, but Wentworth's hands wrapped around a small globular object—and a chill traced its way up his spine. He knew what this was! A bomb filled with the gas of Amoy! That, too, Wentworth stuffed into his pocket and, finally, he found the precious keys!

The eagerness of his hands made it almost impossible to find the locks of his chains and release himself, but finally it was accomplished while the shouts eddied nearer to him. There was a revolver in each fist now, ammunition in his pocket—and on his lips was the Spider's smile! Wentworth reeled to his feet—and paused uncertainly. God help him, blind as he was, he had no idea which way to turn!

Wentworth pressed the back of a hand to his forehead, straining for memory. The car… If he could find the car, he would know which way the banks lay! But where, in the name of heaven, was the car? Fiercely, he concentrated, went back over those moments on the ladder, and the location of the bodies on the ground. Hesitantly, he turned to his right and began a groping shuffling of his uncertain feet. It was maddening, but it seemed impossible to step out boldly. He forced himself to the effort and the perspiration beaded out on his forehead, but he took another step, and another—and bumped against the car! With eager hands, he felt his way to the radiator. Now he knew that the banks to be robbed were off to his left!

HE SWUNG that way, and it took a greater effort of will to step out boldly than it had to attack those three armed guards! He could hear people shouting and fleeing before him. In the distance, a police whistle shrilled. Wentworth swore raggedly. If the police caught him, they would clap him into jail—and once more he would have failed in his attempt to destroy Amoy! But he must warn them of the horror that impended. He must!

He tried to quicken his stride, and something struck hard across his thighs. He lurched forward, and his hands found a park bench… found something else, too, that was human and warm and trembling with terror.

"Don't hurt me, Spider," a small voice pleaded. "Please don't hurt me! I… I'm just a boy, and I'm lame. A lame beggar, Spider!"

Wentworth's hands clutched the boy, and a crazy thought danced across his mind. This was madness—the halt and the blind.

"Son! Lame beggar!" he said gently. "I've never yet hurt a man who didn't deserve it. Son, I'm blind! That's why I fell over you."

The boy's swallow was loud in Wentworth's ears. "Blind," he whispered.

"Listen, son," he said, "and listen carefully. In a few minutes, there's going to be a robbery at the bank over there. I can't face the police. They'll arrest me and… and there's a man I have to… to see at once. You'll have to tell the police, and make them believe…" His voice trailed off at the hopelessness of that request.

The boy said, timidly, "I can't walk, Spider, and the old man took my crutches so I'd have to stay here and play my violin."

Wentworth shook his head, pressed the back of a hand to his forehead. The lame and the blind… He choked the ironic laughter in his throat. "I have legs," he said, "and you have eyes, son. Guide me to a police telephone! The police are coming toward me, and they would destroy their own hope of heaven to get me. Will you lend me your eyes, lame beggar boy?"

The boy said softly, "Sure, Spider. Sure. I… I *like* your face, Spider!"

## THE SPIDER

The laughter came this time, unbidden, to Wentworth's lips, and he lifted the boy to his shoulder.

"Tree ahead, Spider," said the lame boy. "Go to the right. I know where there's a police phone. And Spider, if you could go a little faster? There's a policeman running this way. He's fat, and kind of old. A park policeman, but he's a nice guy, and I wouldn't want...."

"A little to the left," said the boy. "There's a water faucet. To the right... Five more steps and there'll be a curbstone, but there's no traffic in the street. About four inches down...."

Wentworth trotted and the boy's voice ran thinly in his ear....

"That police box is about fifty feet away. A little more to the right. Slow now, only about twenty feet. Steady... *Whoa!*"

Wentworth checked and reached out for the phone.

"At any minute," Wentworth said swiftly, "there will be a concerted attempt to rob the banks on the left side of the Central Square! The bandits will be the same ones who have been blinding people, and they will have bombs to throw among the crowd! Those bombs will blind everyone. For God's sake, get the square cleared, and block the streets around the bank with trucks. Use rifles, if you've got them. I don't think they've tampered with rifle ammunition yet. Have you got that?"

The sergeant's voice came through sharply. "Sure, I've got it, but listen... Wait a minute. Who in the hell are you?"

Wentworth's laughter gusted to his lips unaware. "Don't wait, man! Don't wait... and if you fail—I will come to find out why! This is the Spider speaking!"

He clashed up the phone. He had done what he could to save

the people—and there was another task for the Spider! "Now a dark alley, son," he said swiftly. "There are still things to be done!"

The voice ran on in his ear and presently, answering its orders, Wentworth halted. "This is a dark alley, Spider," said the boy, and his voice was trembling.

Wentworth lifted him down gently. "There is still that man I must see, son," Wentworth said quietly. "We will have to go through city streets, and we are too conspicuous the way we are, but I have a plan. Now tell me, do you know the city?"

"Lived here all my life, Spider!"

Wentworth nodded. "Then think—think hard! Somewhere in this city, there is a firehouse. It is near the water where you can hear the hooting of tugs plainly, and it is near a railway yard, too, for you can hear the switch engines puffing back and forth, and the short signals on their whistles. Think hard, now. That is the place I must find!"

"I'm thinking, sir," the boy answered eagerly. "I know two places where firehouses are near the water, but there's only one where there's a freight yard... I've got it! Cartwright Hook!"

Wentworth smiled grimly, "I recently acquired a little money," he said. "Not much, for it seems my guards were underpaid. But enough to get us to Cartwright Hook... by taxi! Come now, my eyes, out of this alley, and to the nearest taxi stand. We are beggars, if anyone asks—an old musician and his boy with a tin cup. Wait, I must take off this cape. Is it out of sight under my coat? Good! Now, we must give this hat a jauntier air."

The boy said, timidly, "Please, sir, there's a sign on your hat!"

"A sign?" Wentworth's voice tautened.

"Yes, sir. It says… it says…."

"Go on, say!"

"It says, 'The Spider died a coward. Long live Amoy!'"

Wentworth's lips stretched thinly, and he fumbled the card from the band of his hat. "Why, thanks, son," he said, and strain was in his voice, "and now we must be on our way." He put the card inside his coat, where he could find it again, and picked up the small boy to rest him on his shoulder, tucked the violin under his arm. "Lead on, my eyes!"

THE TAXI driver demurred until Wentworth handed money to the boy for the fare, then he got underway grumblingly. He could see no tip in this trip.

"Promise him a dollar for speed, son," Wentworth said softly, "if there is enough in that roll!"

"There's plenty, sir, and my name is Joe."

Wentworth heard once more the rush and rumble of traffic, and felt the cold pressure of speed-wind on his face. His hands strayed to the revolvers at his belt, touched the round hard lump of a bomb in his pocket. Grimness grew upon his mouth.

"We are there, sir. The fire-engine house is right down the street."

Wentworth nodded. "About a block beyond that have the driver stop."

When the taxi slid to a halt, Wentworth leaned forward. "Driver," he said. "This whole roll is yours, for two more slight favors. Somewhere in this block is a saloon with a basement where crooks meet a lot. It's not much of a place on the outside, and it stinks of stale beer and staler smoke. There's a poolroom behind it, where you can hear the balls clicking to all hours of the night, and once or twice there has been shooting there over a poker game—but the police never came. You tell me where that place is, and after you have set me down in front of it, you take this boy to the nearest police station, but not too quickly. Do these things and the roll is yours."

The driver twisted around and stared into the blind, roughly bearded face of the Spider, took in the hard set of the lips. " 'Tis a funny thing you're asking," he said, "but you've described the place to a T. It's Michavelli's in the next block there, and it's third from the corner."

"Wait," Wentworth said. "Joe, describe it to me."

"There are two doors, sir," Joe said rapidly. "There's one right near this end of the building, with steps that go down—but I can't see how many—and there's another entrance with swing doors, and that has one step about three inches high. The windows have dark-green paint across them in a wide stripe, but you can see over it all right. The windows are dirty."

"It's the basement door I'll want," Wentworth said softly. "Will I bump my head going down?"

"Not with me to guide you, sir!" Joe cried.

Wentworth shook his head. "No, I go in here alone, Joe. And you go to the police station with the driver and tell them what has happened. Tell them that Amoy is in that basement, and tell them…" He drew out the cape and threw it about his shoulders, dragged the hat low over his blind eyes. "Tell them that the Spider has gone there, too! Driver, stop in front of the basement door!"

Joe said timidly, "If you took my violin, sir, they might think... they might think you were a beggar!"

Wentworth turned his head and his smile was very gentle. "Joe, if I come out of this, you'll have the finest violin that money can buy."

The taxi driver said, "Look, I don't know what this is all about but what I've heard of you, Spider. You're a right guy. You're asking for it, going down there."

Wentworth nodded slowly, "Yes, that's right," he said, and grimness crept into his voice. "Drive on! *I'm asking for it!*"

"There are seven steps, sir," Joe whispered, "and you'll have to duck your head a little. And about five steps along the hall, there's a door on your left with a little hole in the middle of it, covered by a slide."

Wentworth nodded his thanks, but said no more. He couldn't find the voice for kind words, for there was death in his heart. There was death in his stride, too, as he moved across the walk. Presently, word would come to Amoy that his plans had failed again, thanks to the Spider, and before that time he must be inside. He must hear Amoy when he cried out his rage. His foot slipped on the edge of the top step, and he caught himself by an effort, went down slowly with the violin tucked under one arm.

## CHAPTER 11
## THE SPIDER'S HOUR

HE WENT down the steps, and paused at their bottom. The taxi had already shot off down the street, and there was another machine stopping at the curb. Feet skated across the sidewalk, plunged down the steps. Wentworth was roughly shouldered aside, and fists beat on the door.

"Open up, for the love of heaven!" the man gasped. "Open up, or we're gone!"

Wentworth heard the door wrench open, and the man blunder through. He wedged his foot across the threshold and the slammed door caught on it and vibrated open again. The Spider slipped inside, stood with his back against the wall, his head bent above the violin while he listened with painful concentration. Behind him, he bolted the door!

"Amoy!" the man was shouting. Amoy! The Spider got away! Warned the police! They bottled us up, damn them, shot us down like flies! Yes, *shot us down!* Damn it, I tell you there were cops there from New York City with some kind of guns that would poke a hole through three men at once, and they mowed us down!"

Wentworth's lips twisted in grim delight, and his hand slipped into his pocket. He could hear the squeak of Amoy's voice coming nearer now; the pad of his feet along a hallway.

Wentworth's hand closed about the bomb. It was a fearsome thing to use, but there was need to even the odds here... and there was no man here who was not an ally of Amoy, else the news would not have been shouted like that. No man here but had joyed in the easy money to be gained by blinding a few hundred persons!

Wentworth waited until he heard Amoy's voice squeaking

with rage nearby, until he knew that Amoy was close. Then, the Spider's voice boomed out in the low-ceilinged room.

*"Long live Amoy!"*

And he threw the bomb!

When it burst, Wentworth was already leaping sideways. A table crashed from his path. Chairs slammed to the floor and already there were shouts of agony. But Wentworth had a set goal, and he raced along the wall with a hand sliding against it until he reached the inner door through which Amoy had entered. Then, carefully, he laid the violin on the floor beside him, slid to his knees and took out the two guns he had wrested from the guards. He twisted his head and listened to the timbre of the voices. When he had spotted the one he sought, he began to shoot....

WHEN THE police came rushing to the scene, summoned by Joe, there was no sound at all from the basement of the saloon, and no one in the room above. The cops plunged down the steps and their eyes were shielded by sealed goggles, and at their head ran a broad-jawed man whose gray eyes glinted fire through the goggles. Behind him was another, heavily-built man whose bare head was close-clipped, and whose chest and shoulders were those of a bull.

"I'll go first, Kade," this man said sharply.

"It may be dangerous, Commissioner," cried Henry Kade.

But Commissioner Sanford Dane, of New York City, shouldered past him and threw his weight against the door and it slammed wide open. Kade bolted through the door with a questing, thin-snouted automatic of foreign make in his fist. There were seven bodies scattered on the floor, and at sight of one of them, a great tub of a man flattened now in death, a grimly satisfied smile crept across Henry Kade's mouth.

From his left, a voice called faintly, "Oh, if you are men, help me, help me! Oh, the screams! The guns!"

Commissioner Dane swore and swung that way. Huddled in a dark corner, the twisted figure of a man was crouched over a violin. There was a matted beard on his face, and his hair was wild, and the clothing he wore was ragged. In three long strides, the commissioner reached the man, jerked him to his feet.

"Who are you?" he growled. "What happened here?"

The man shivered, and his shoulders cringed, and he clutched his violin more closely to him. "I don't know," he whimpered. "Oh, I don't know. I came in here to play for a little money. I'm a beggar, sir, and somebody opened the door and laughed. God, I hope I never hear a laugh like that again! And he cried, '*Long live Amoy!*' And then there were screams and shots, and I don't know, sir. Truly, I don't." The beggar lifted his head, and blind eyes rolled in their sockets, horribly. "You see, sir, I'm *blind!*"

Dane turned away with an oath as Kade shouted to him. "Here's the answer, sir. That boy told a straight story. See, on the mirror!"

On the mirror behind the bar, there was a crudely printed sign. It read, "The Spider is a coward. Long live Amoy!" And over and around it, there was scrawled a great erratic spider, and it had been drawn in blood.

Dane cursed savagely as he read it aloud and, against the

wall, the blind beggar huddled over his violin and listened with caught breath.

Wentworth waited and heard only Dane's hoarse, nonplussed swearing. Feet strode toward Wentworth and he played once more his cringing role, felt a hard hand jerk his chin up, and heard the flare of a match being struck.

Dane's voice came out harshly, "The man's blind as a bat. His eyes don't react to light. Not even the Spider could come into a place like this, blind... and kill seven men!"

Wentworth waited tensely, waited for Kade to speak. He heard Kade.

"You're absolutely right, Commissioner," he said with conviction. "Not even the Spider!"

And presently, Kade's hand was on his arm, lifting him to his feet. "You might as well wait outside, beggar man," Kade said quietly. "This gas might hurt even those blind eyes of yours..." There was a tenderness in his voice like a woman's, and there was gentleness in the touch of his hand. "You heard a great man speak here today, and you heard a great man use his guns. If ever you hear that voice again, blind beggar man, you say to the speaker that Hank Kade says this, 'The Spider is not a man. He's closer to the blessed saints!'"

NOW WENTWORTH was on the pavement outside, stumbling blindly along, with the violin clutched under his arm, and there was despair in his heart. He had performed his task, and, a thing he had not expected—he was alive and free! Free, but *blind.* And in New York, the police would be waiting for Richard Wentworth, or for the Spider, and his pockets were empty.

Wentworth tucked the violin beneath his chin, and the bow touched softly as he brought the strings to harmony. Well, get on with it, blind beggar, play your little tune, and hold out your hat for pennies. It's all you're good for, Richard Wentworth! The Spider should have died there in that cellar while glory was upon him, not lived to beg for pennies!

"Yes, yes," Dane's voice was impatient now. "I know all about the Spider's genius for disguise, and I know there are stories that he is blind. But I tell you no blind man could go into that cellar and kill seven men… and walk out unharmed! The blindness of the Spider is a lot of ridiculous propaganda!"

The bitter laughter rose to Wentworth's lips and he made the violin squawk to hide it. Propaganda, these poor sightless eyes! The tune he played was—*"The Three Blind Mice!"*

At the entrance to the saloon, Dane checked his curses to stare toward the beggar musician, jerked his head impatiently. "Throw a cordon around this neighborhood, damn it! I want the Spider found! I'll see him burn in the electric chair if it's the last thing I ever do!"

Wentworth's violin jerked and danced to the lilting music, but there was no laughter in his heart… and he heard a thin voice call to him softly, the voice of the boy, Joe.

"Please, sir," he whispered. "Please, I have a message for you! Lift me up!" Wentworth stopped his savage self-mockery in music, and stooped to grope for the boy, found his uplifted hand and swung him to his shoulder.

"Guide me, Joe!" he whispered, and stumbled off along the street, and policemen stood aside with pitying sidelong glances.

Joe was stooping toward Wentworth's ears. "Around the corner, sir—a lady in a car."

Wentworth's head jerked up. "No!" he said sharply. *"No!"*

God, not that! He could not go to Nita with these poor blind eyes. Oh, she would welcome him, but....

"A *blind* lady in a car!" said Joe.

Wentworth felt his heart tighten in his chest, and there was no beating in it at all. He felt a faintness like death crowd into his skull. Nita... Nita *blind!* He began to run, stumblingly, and the words of Joe in his ear, guiding him, were a thing he did not hear at all, and yet obeyed. He ran clear of the walls and he rounded the corner, and brought up hard against the side of the car.

"Nita!" he gasped. "Nita, dear, your eyes...."

Nita's laughter, coming to his ears, was sweet as always, and her hands were soft on his own. "Dick—oh, *Dick!*"

Wentworth stumbled into the car, with the boy, Joe, in his arms, but the horror still coiled in his breast.

The car glided forward softly and Nita's hands were twined with his. "I am not unhappy," she said quietly. "Now, we have each other, dearest. Now, you cannot battle any more...."

Wentworth shook his head, and his lips grew thin in his worn face. "I still can fight," he said roughly. "The Spider proved that tonight. There is no ending that way, Nita, not until...."

Nita sighed, and her voice lifted. "Of course not, Dick," she said steadily. "I was a fool to try you so. Dick, I shall see again. My eyes are bandaged, but the doctor is sure of ultimate cure, and since you used those palliative drops, *your* eyes can be healed also."

"*See* again?" Wentworth stammered. "I may see again? Why then… Why then, I am glad I did not die back there. I am glad…" His hands groped for Nita's and found them in the darkness.

"Hey!" Joe whispered. "Hey! There's a man coming toward the car!"

Wentworth tautened… but there was no proof here that he was the Spider.

"Joe," he said softly. "My life is in your hands. Don't mention that I am… the Spider!"

"I'll cut out my tongue first!" Joe said fiercely. "Listen, this man walks with a cane, and he leans on it. I think he's a tall man, and he has a pointed mustache and his face is awful thin…."

Wentworth sucked in a quick breath. "Has he… Has he a flower in his buttonhole?" he asked quickly.

"Gosh, can you see?" Joe asked. "You're right. He has. He…."

Nita whispered, "Oh, Dick! *It's Stanley Kirkpatrick!*"

Nita's hands were straining tightly against his, and Wentworth felt his heart swell. He said quietly. "Nita, this may be the end. It may be… Who's at the wheel of this car?"

Before Nita could reply, a man's grave crisp voice answered for her. "Ram Singh, of course, Dick, but there is no need for you to fly."

Wentworth blew out a slow breath, and his voice was quiet. "Kirkpatrick!" he said. "Stanley, old man, I thought the doctors had given you up these many clays. I'm glad to hear your voice again, even if it means…."

"What, Dick?"

"If it means my arrest on that asinine charge of murder that Dane has been pressing against me!" Wentworth said shortly. "I haven't a chance to clear myself in court until I get my vision again, until I can work on the case…."

Kirkpatrick laughed softly. Wentworth heard the laboring of his breath as he climbed into the car.

"I'm relieving Dane as commissioner of police tonight," Kirkpatrick said quietly. "I'm taking back my job from that ass. And there is no need of your clearing yourself of that charge you so justly term ridiculous! The Spider has long ago killed the man who blew up those brave officers at your home, and you did your best to save them. The doctors just let the news of it get through to me, curse them! Dick, you're a free man!"

"Free…" Wentworth echoed the word softly. Free, yes, to battle against fresh enemies of mankind, and once more with the resources of his wealth at his command! He could fight better now… until his good fortune failed him, and this same Kirkpatrick, who freed him now so gladly, slammed shut the cell doors upon the Spider! But until that time, they would be warm friends, and gallant secret enemies. And Nita was beside him, her hand warm in his….

Wentworth laughed softly. He groped in the darkness, and found Joe's shoulder. "Kirk," he said. "I want you to meet a friend of mine—a boy who is going to be the greatest violinist that the world's best teachers can turn out!"

# THE SPIDER AND THE EYELESS LEGION

Joe said, "Gee! Oh, *gee!*"

**BACK ON** the sidewalk before the saloon, the man who soon would be only ex-commissioner Sanford Dane was glaring sourly at the darkness. He whirled to peer where the blind beggar had stood, the beggar who had played so beautifully a simple tune that was mocking to his ears... Why, damn it, the Spider was a master musician, a virtuoso of the violin—and no blind beggar played like that!

Dane shouted out hoarsely. "Find that beggar! Find him quickly! We've let the Spider slip through our fingers."

Behind his back, Detective Sergeant Henry Kade smiled dourly. He echoed the commissioner's orders, but he had seen Joe lifted to the Spider's shoulder, had seen him run... Kade's grin broadened. Softly, almost against his will, Kade began to whistle—and the tune he whistled was, *"The Three Blind Mice!"*

"Damn you, Kade!" Dane shouted. "Stop whistling that infernal tune!"

It must have been imagination, Kade knew, but he was almost sure he could hear an echo of a laugh—the echo of the Spider's mocking laughter!

## THE SPIDER

❏ #1: The Spider Strikes — $13.95
❏ #2: The Wheel of Death — $13.95
❏ #3: Wings of the Black Death — $13.95
❏ #4: City of Flaming Shadows — $13.95
❏ #5: Empire of Doom! — $13.95
❏ #6: Citadel of Hell — $13.95
❏ #7: The Serpent of Destruction — $13.95
❏ #8: The Mad Horde — $13.95
❏ #9: Satan's Death Blast — $13.95
❏ #10: The Corpse Cargo — $13.95
❏ #11: Prince of the Red Looters — $13.95
❏ #12: Reign of the Silver Terror — $13.95
❏ #13: Builders of the Dark Empire — $13.95
❏ #14: Death's Crimson Juggernaut — $13.95
❏ #15: The Red Death Rain — $13.95
❏ #16: The City Destroyer — $13.95
❏ #17: The Pain Emperor — $13.95
❏ #18: The Flame Master — $13.95
❏ #19: Slaves of the Crime Master — $13.95
❏ #20: Reign of the Death Fiddler — $13.95
❏ #21: Hordes of the Red Butcher — $13.95
❏ #22: Dragon Lord of the Underworld — $13.95
❏ #23: Master of the Death-Madness — $13.95
❏ #24: King of the Red Killers — $13.95
❏ #25: Overlord of the Damned — $13.95
❏ #26: Death Reign of the Vampire King — $13.95
❏ #27: Emperor of the Yellow Death — $13.95
❏ #28: The Mayor of Hell — $13.95
❏ #29: Slaves of the Murder Syndicate — $13.95
❏ #30: Green Globes of Death — $13.95
❏ #31: The Cholera King — $13.95
❏ #32: Slaves of the Dragon — $13.95
❏ #33: Legions of Madness — $12.95
❏ #34: Laboratory of the Damned — $12.95
❏ #35: Satan's Sightless Legion — $12.95
❏ #36: The Coming of the Terror — $12.95
❏ #37: The Devil's Death-Dwarfs — $12.95
❏ #38: City of Dreadful Night — $12.95
❏ #39: Reign of the Snake Men — $12.95
❏ #40: Dictator of the Damned — $12.95
❏ #41: The Mill-Town Massacres — $12.95
❏ #42: Satan's Workshop — $12.95
❏ #43: Scourge of the Yellow Fangs — $12.95
❏ #44: The Devil's Pawnbroker — $12.95
❏ #45: Voyage of the Coffin Ship — $12.95
❏ #46: The Man Who Ruled in Hell — $13.95
❏ #47: Slaves of the Black Monarch — $13.95
❏ #48: Machineguns Over the White House $13.95
❏ #49: The City That Dared Not Eat — $13.95
❏ #50: Master of the Flaming Horde — $13.95
❏ #51: Satan's Switchboard — $13.95
❏ #52: Legions of the Accursed Light — $13.95
❏ #53: The City of Lost Men — $13.95
❏ #54: The Grey Horde Creeps — $13.95
❏ #55: City of Whispering Death — $13.95
❏ #56: When Thousands Slept in Hell — $13.95
❏ #57: Satan's Shakles — $14.95
❏ #58: The Emperor From Hell — $14.95
❏ #59: The Devil's Candlesticks — $14.95
❏ #60: The City That Paid to Die — $14.95
❏ #61: The Spider at Bay — $14.95
❏ #62: Scourge of the Black Legions — $14.95
❏ #63: The Withering Death — $14.95
❏ #64: Claws of the Golden Dragon — $14.95
❏ #65: The Song of Death — $14.95
❏ #66: The Silver Death Reign — $14.95
❏ #67: Blight of the Blazing Eye — $14.95
❏ #68: King of the Fleshless Legion — $14.95
❏ #69: Rule of the Monster Men — $16.95
❏ #70: The Spider and the Slaves of Hell — $16.95
❏ #71: The Spider and the Fire God — $16.95
❏ #72: The Corpse Broker — $16.95
❏ *NEW:* #73: The Spider and the Eyeless Legion
— $16.95

## THE WESTERN RAIDER

❏ #1: Guns of the Damned — $13.95
❏ #2: The Hawk Rides Back from Death — $13.95
❏ #3: Gun-Call for the Lost Legion — $13.95
❏ #4: The Law of Silver Trent — $13.95
❏ #5: The Gun-Prayer of Silver Trent — $13.95
❏ #6: Silver Trent Rides Alone — $13.95

## G-8 AND HIS BATTLE ACES

❏ #1: The Bat Staffel — $13.95

## CAPTAIN SATAN

❏ #1: The Mask of the Damned — $13.95
❏ #2: Parole for the Dead — $13.95
❏ #3: The Dead Man Express — $13.95
❏ #4: A Ghost Rides the Dawn — $13.95
❏ #5: The Ambassador From Hell — $13.95

## DR. YEN SIN

❏ #1: Mystery of the Dragon's Shadow — $12.95
❏ #2: Mystery of the Golden Skull — $12.95
❏ #3: Mystery of the Singing Mummies — $12.95

### ACE G-MAN
- ❏ #1: The Suicide Squad Reports for Death — $14.95
- ❏ #2: Coffins for the Suicide Squad — $14.95
- ❏ #3: Shells for the Suicide Squad — $14.95
- ❏ #4: The Suicide Squad in Corpse-Town — $14.95
- ❏ #5: Wanted–In Three Pine Coffins — $14.95
- ❏ #6: The Suicide Squad's Dawn Patrol — $14.95
- ❏ #7: Targets for the Flaming Arrow — $16.95

### OPERATOR 5
- ❏ #1: The Masked Invasion — $13.95
- ❏ #2: The Invisible Empire — $13.95
- ❏ #3: The Yellow Scourge — $13.95
- ❏ #4: The Melting Death — $13.95
- ❏ #5: Cavern of the Damned — $13.95
- ❏ #6: Master of Broken Men — $13.95
- ❏ #7: Invasion of the Dark Legions — $13.95
- ❏ #8: The Green Death Mists — $13.95
- ❏ #9: Legions of Starvation — $13.95
- ❏ #10: The Red Invader — $13.95
- ❏ #11: The League of War-Monsters — $13.95
- ❏ #12: The Army of the Dead — $13.95
- ❏ #13: March of the Flame Marauders — $13.95
- ❏ #14: Blood Reign of the Dictator — $13.95
- ❏ #15: Invasion of the Yellow Warlords — $13.95
- ❏ #16: Legions of the Death Master — $13.95
- ❏ #17: Hosts of the Flaming Death — $13.95
- ❏ #18: Invasion of the Crimson Death Cult — $13.95
- ❏ #19: Attack of the Blizzard Men — $13.95
- ❏ #20: Scourge of the Invisible Death — $13.95
- ❏ #21: Raiders of the Red Death — $13.95
- ❏ #22: War-Dogs of the Green Destroyer — $13.95
- ❏ #23: Rockets From Hell — $13.95
- ❏ #24: War-Masters from the Orient — $13.95
- ❏ #25: Crime's Reign of Terror — $13.95
- ❏ #26: Death's Ragged Army — $13.95
- ❏ #27: Patriots' Death Battalion — $13.95
- ❏ #28: The Bloody Forty-five Days — $13.95
- ❏ #29: America's Plague Battalions — $13.95
- ❏ #30: Liberty's Suicide Legions — $13.95
- ❏ #31: Siege of the Thousand Patriots — $13.95
- ❏ #32: Patriots' Death March — $14.95
- ❏ #33: Revolt of the Lost Legions — $14.95
- ❏ #34: Drums of Destruction — $14.95
- ❏ #35: The Army Without a Country — $14.95
- ❏ #36: The Bloody Frontiers — $14.95
- ❏ #37: The Coming of the Mongol Hordes — $14.95
- ❏ #38: The Siege That Brought Black Death — $16.95
- ❏ #39: Revolt of the Devil Men — $16.95
- ❏ *NEW:* #40: The Suicide Battalion — $16.95

### RED FINGER
- ❏ #1: Second-Hand Death — $24.95

### THE MASKED MARKSMAN
- ❏ #1: Death Takes an Encore — $16.95

### CAPTAIN COMBAT
- ❏ #1: The Sky Beast of Berlin — $13.95
- ❏ #2: Red Wings For the Blood Battalion — $13.95
- ❏ #3: Low Ceiling For Nazi Hell Hawks — $13.95

### DUSTY AYRES AND HIS BATTLE BIRDS
- ❏ #1: Black Lightning! — $13.95
- ❏ #2: Crimson Doom — $13.95
- ❏ #3: The Purple Tornado — $13.95
- ❏ #4: The Screaming Eye — $13.95
- ❏ #5: The Green Thunderbolt — $13.95
- ❏ #6: The Red Destroyer — $13.95
- ❏ #7: The White Death — $13.95
- ❏ #8: The Black Avenger — $13.95
- ❏ #9: The Silver Typhoon — $13.95
- ❏ #10: The Troposphere F-S — $13.95
- ❏ #11: The Blue Cyclone — $13.95
- ❏ #12: The Tesla Raiders — $13.95

### MAVERICKS
- ❏ #1: Five Against the Law — $12.95
- ❏ #2: Mesquite Manhunters — $12.95
- ❏ #3: Bait for the Lobo Pack — $12.95
- ❏ #4: Doc Grimson's Outlaw Posse — $12.95
- ❏ #5: Charlie Parr's Gunsmoke Cure — $12.95

### THE MYSTERIOUS WU FANG
- ❏ #1: The Case of the Six Coffins — $12.95
- ❏ #2: The Case of the Scarlet Feather — $12.95
- ❏ #3: The Case of the Yellow Mask — $12.95
- ❏ #4: The Case of the Suicide Tomb — $12.95
- ❏ #5: The Case of the Green Death — $12.95
- ❏ #6: The Case of the Black Lotus — $12.95
- ❏ #7: The Case of the Hidden Scourge — $12.95

### THE SECRET 6
- ❏ #1: The Red Shadow — $13.95
- ❏ #2: House of Walking Corpses — $13.95
- ❏ #3: The Monster Murders — $13.95
- ❏ #4: The Golden Alligator — $13.95

### CAPTAIN ZERO
- ❏ #1: City of Deadly Sleep — $13.95
- ❏ #2: The Mark of Zero! — $13.95
- ❏ #3: The Golden Murder Syndicate — $13.95